BOARDING SCHOOL MYSTERIES

poisoned

Other books in the growing Faithgirlz!™ Library

Boarding School Mysteries
Vanished (Book One)
Betrayed (Book Two)
Burned (Book Three)

The Sophie Series
Sophie's World (Book One)
Sophie's Secret (Book Two)
Sophie Under Pressure (Book Three)
Sophie Steps Up (Book Four)
Sophie's First Dance (Book Five)
Sophie's Stormy Summer (Book Six)
Sophie's Friendship Fiasco (Book Seven)
Sophie and the New Girl (Book Eight)
Sophie Flakes Out (Book Nine)
Sophie Loves Jimmy (Book Ten)
Sophie's Drama (Book Eleven)
Sophie Gets Real (Book Twelve)

The Lucy Series
Lucy Doesn't Wear Pink (Book One)
Lucy Out of Bounds (Book Two)
Lucy's "Perfect" Summer (Book Three)
Lucy Finds Her Way (Book Four)

Other books by Kristi Holl
What's A Girl to Do?
Shine on, Girl!: Devotions to Keep You Sparkling
Girlz Rock: Devotions for You
Chick Chat: More Devotions for Girls
No Boys Allowed: Devotions for Girls

Check out www.faithgirlz.com

faith*girlz*

BOARDING SCHOOL MYSTERIES

poisoned

Formerly titled *Pick Your Poison*

Kristi Holl

ZONDERKIDZ

Poisoned
Copyright © 2008, 2011 by Kristi Holl
Formerly titled *Pick Your Poison*

This title is also available as a Zondervan ebook.
Visit www.zondervan.com/ebooks.

Requests for information should be addressed to:
Zonderkidz, 3900 *Sparks Drive SE, Grand Rapids, Michigan 49546*

Library of Congress Cataloging-in-Publication Data
Holl, Kristi.
    [Pick your poison]
    Poisoned / by Kristi Holl.
       p. cm. — (Faithgirlz) (Boarding school mysteries ; bk. 4)
    Originally published in 2008 under the title, Pick your poison.
    ISBN 978-0-310-72095-9 (softcover)
    [1. Boarding schools—Fiction. 2. Schools—Fiction. 3. Poisons—Fiction.
    4. Christian life—Fiction. 5. Mystery and detective stories.] I. Title.
    PZ7.H7079Poi   20118
    {Fic}—dc22
                                                      2010037926

Art direction and cover design: Sarah Molegraaf
Interior design: Carlos Eluterio Estrada

So we fix our eyes not on what is seen, but what is unseen.
For what is seen is temporary, but what is unseen is eternal.
— 2 Corinthians 4:18

table of contents

1	Sneak Attack	7
2	Poisoning	21
3	Storm Warning	29
4	Danger, Warning, Caution	41
5	Poison Potatoes	53
6	Creepy Crawlies	63
7	Caught in the Act	77
8	Setting a Trap	89
9	Backfired	99
10	Safe at Last	113

1

sneak attack

Birthday parties were supposed to be fun, but that warm Saturday evening, nothing went as Jeri McKane expected. Illness was the last thing on her mind as a cardinal whistled outside her open window. She had no clue that in two short hours her friends would be poisoned.

Jeri twisted from side to side in front of the mirror. "What's wrong with how I look?" she asked her roommate. Her dark blue shirt complemented both her jeans and the denim flats with red bows.

"What's *wrong* with it?" Rosa Sanchez peered over her shoulder. "It looks like something your mom would wear." Rosa always looked cool—like now, in her short denim skirt and tee with a fuzzy pink scarf. Her black waist-length hair made any outfit look awesome. "Want to borrow something?" she asked with a wink. "Don't forget, Dallas is coming tonight. What if he brings some cutie with him and you look like that?"

Dallas. Jeri's heart skipped a beat, and she turned her back to Rosa to hide the blush that flooded her face. Dallas Chandler, a boy from their church, attended the Patterson School for Boys on the other side of Landmark Hills. So far, Jeri had done a good job of hiding her crush on him. She refused to risk Rosa telling Dallas about her feelings. Before Christmas, Rosa had done that to a boy Abby liked, and Abby had nearly died of shame.

"How about this?" Rosa held up a lavender top with a lace edge. Then she grabbed a short black skirt from her closet. "Or this?"

"Hmm." It was tempting, even if it was awfully short. "I suppose I could wear tights with it."

"No way, José!" Rosa shook her head. "Show off those legs!" She frowned. "You're awfully white though. You have any of that bronze gel stuff?"

"No." Jeri glanced at her watch. "Anyway, I gotta get downstairs. I'm setting tables for Abby."

Tonight, Abby Wright, the girl from England who lived in the dorm room next to theirs, was fixing a meal for eight people. It was her home ec project, and it included a birthday cake for another sixth grader who lived there in Hampton House. Since part of her grade was based on proper boy/girl etiquette at a dinner, Dallas and a friend had agreed to show up and lend a hand.

Just then, heavy footsteps pounded up the stairs, and Jeri whipped around as their door burst open. Nikki Brown's face was beaded with sweat. "Come quick! Both of you."

"What's the matter?" Jeri asked.

"You know Abby's tuna turnovers? A tube of biscuits exploded!"

Jeri gasped. "No way!"

"It was sitting on the stove while the oven preheated."

"I saw something like that on TV," Rosa said. "Groceries were left in a car parked in the sun. It got so hot the cans of biscuits exploded all over the car."

"Exactly." Nikki rolled her eyes. "The grocery store's delivery guy is busy, so Ms. Carter's driving Abby there for more biscuits." Nikki flicked some lettuce off her fringed leather vest. "I was making the salad, but now I have to clean up the biscuit glop. I can't do everything!"

"We'll help," Jeri said. "Is the birthday cake okay?"

"Sorta. A flying biscuit mashed some of the frosting."

"I'll fix the cake." Rosa put on a pink ball cap with a silver band. "Nikki, you clean up the biscuit mess. Jeri's setting the tables."

"Okay, but hurry up. Those guys get here in half an hour." Nikki's cowboy boots clomped back down the stairs.

Jeri turned back to the mirror. Should she wear the skirt or shouldn't she? In the mirror's reflection, she spotted the desktop photo of her and her mom sitting on their porch swing back home in Iowa. Her mom's trusting smile made her hesitate. And yet, if she was old enough to go to school halfway across the country, wasn't she old enough to dress herself without Mom's advice? If only the skirt weren't quite so short ...

Jeri handed Rosa's skirt back. "Thanks, anyway." She yanked a comb through her shoulder-length brown hair, added a headband, and followed Rosa down the steps.

"Weird to have the dorm so quiet tonight," Rosa said.

Jeri nodded. Most of the girls were eating supper in the dining hall. Miss Barbara, their assistant house mother, planned to take them roller skating afterward. Only Emily — the birthday girl — and her roommate, Brooke, were still upstairs in their room, waiting for Abby's dinner.

Downstairs, the kitchen was a disaster. Globs of sticky biscuit dough stuck to the floor, the table, the stove, and the windowsill. One biscuit had mashed a yellow frosting rose and the green *y* from *Birthday*. Rosa immediately went to work on the cake.

Nikki was on the floor scraping up pieces of canned biscuits. The makings for the turnover filling — tuna, shredded cheese, ripe olives, and hardboiled eggs — were on the counter, waiting to be mixed and wrapped inside biscuit dough. *Poor Abby!* Jeri thought as she went to set the tables and arrange flowers.

Down the hall, two card tables and eight chairs were already set up in the first-floor study room. Disposable items — bright yellow paper tablecloths, plates, and cups, plus plastic silverware — were in a sack beside the door. Jeri quickly set both tables.

Also by the door was a huge bouquet of yellow daffodils with orange centers, enough flowers for two centerpieces. She breathed deeply; she *loved* that smell. Using the sharp knife lying there, she followed Abby's written instructions to cut an inch off each stem before putting the flowers in vases.

As she worked, she allowed herself to pretend that the flowers were *hers*, and Dallas had surprised her with them. "Just to celebrate spring," he might say, giving her that slow Southern grin and a wink.

"Are you done?" Nikki called from the doorway, making her jump.

"Ow!" Jeri dropped the knife. A thin red line appeared on her thumb, and blood dripped onto a daffodil. "Get me a Band-Aid, will you?"

Nikki dashed off and reappeared with the kitchen's first-aid kit. She wiped Jeri's cut and applied disinfectant cream and a Band-Aid. "You okay?" At Jeri's nod, Nikki headed back to the kitchen. Jeri finished the bouquets, tossing the stems and the bloom with her blood on it into the garbage.

In the kitchen, Jeri found things more under control. Rosa had fixed the *y* on top of the cake and removed the flattened rose. The biscuits were in the wastebasket. Nikki was breaking fresh mushrooms into small pieces for the salad, while Rosa grated a carrot to add. The filling for the turnovers still needed to be mixed.

"Should I go ahead—" Jeri was cut off as Abby and the house mother rushed in the back door.

Abby's gaze darted around the room, then she visibly relaxed. "You guys are the best mates!" She set a new can of biscuits onto the counter. "Thank you!" After shrugging off her jacket, she dumped the ingredients into a mixing bowl.

Jeri gave Abby's shoulder a quick squeeze. "Everything else is done. Can I help with the turnovers while you get dressed?"

"I wish!" Abby tucked her wind-blown blonde hair behind her ears. "I can have helpers for everything but the main dish. I have to cook it by myself."

"While I take photos for proof," Ms. Carter said, clicking away with her camera.

"Wait, Jer, can you do something else for me?" Abby asked, stirring her ingredients together. "Have Emily and Brooke come downstairs now. Then, when the guys arrive, you take them into the living room and serve the hors d'oeuvres."

"You're having hors d'oeuvres?" Jeri smiled, but her stomach tightened. She didn't want to be in charge. What if she dumped the snacks into Dallas's lap? "What do you want me to serve?"

"Tortilla swirls and Asian meatballs—they're in the fridge." Abby nodded toward a cupboard. "In there are some colored toothpicks. They're for dipping the meatballs in the sweet-and-sour sauce."

"You're making my mouth water!"

"Good." Abby grinned. "Tell that to my home ec teacher. You'll love those swirls. They're tortillas filled with cream cheese and salsa, then rolled up and sliced like little pinwheels." She flattened a canned biscuit, spooned tuna mixture into the center, folded the dough over, and pinched the edges together with a fork. "I'll change clothes while the turnovers bake."

Fifteen minutes later the front doorbell sounded. Jeri checked her reflection in the mirror over the fireplace, took a deep breath, and started down the short hallway.

Rosa came from behind, stepped around her, and opened the door with a flourish. Flashing a bright smile, she ushered the boys in. "Welcome to Hampton House," she said.

Dallas spotted Jeri and grinned. "Hi." He hung his cowboy hat on the hall tree. Jeri didn't know which was shinier—his polished boots or his silver belt buckle. "You all know Jonathan?" he asked, hooking a thumb at his friend.

Jonathan mumbled "Hello." His red tracksuit swished as he tossed his ball cap onto one of the hooks.

Rosa stepped between the boys and slipped her arms through theirs. "Let me introduce you to the birthday girl." She led them to the living room, where Emily softly played a song by heart on the piano. "Meet Emily Kirkland," Rosa said.

"Hi, Emily," Dallas said. "And happy birthday!"

"Thanks." Emily's smile transformed her plain round face. Dressed in tan Bermudas and a brown shirt, she almost blended into the wood paneling. "That's my room-mate, Brooke."

"Hey." Brooke stood framed by the picture window, poised as if waiting to have her photo taken. In her cropped jacket, plaid capris, and sequined flip-flops, she could have been a model. *She must love those capris*, Jeri thought. It looked like she'd outgrown them a while back. Then again, most of Rosa's capris were skin tight, and they were brand new.

Rosa tuned the radio to her favorite music station, and then turned to Jeri. "Wanna get the snacks? I mean, the hors d'oeuvres? Tell Nikki to bring in sodas too." She perched on the arm of the couch beside Dallas, her swinging legs barely covered by her short skirt. "I'll take care of our guests."

"Sure." Jeri turned, wishing now that she *had* borrowed the skirt. Rosa was getting all the attention, and her bossiness was irritating. Who left *her* in charge?

Jeri passed around the hors d'oeuvres, and she was grateful when Brooke offered to help refill people's glasses. Finally Abby came downstairs. "Hi, everybody. I think it's all ready." She headed to the study room. "Follow me. One guy per table, okay?"

"Relax, everybody," the house mother added from the hall where she waited with her camera.

Jeri's heart fluttered. Now what? Would Dallas ask her to sit at his table?

The boys grinned and split up. Rosa, Emily, and Brooke hurried to Dallas's table. Disappointed, Jeri followed Nikki and Abby to Jonathan's table. Very nice, very quiet Jonathan. The boys seated each of the girls before sitting down themselves. Ms. Carter's camera clicked away.

Jeri couldn't remember the last time she'd felt so stiff and awkward. She knew this was all part of Abby's requirement for a good grade, but it felt so silly. She sneaked a glance at Abby, waiting for her to unfold her perfect fan-shaped napkin. Next to her, apparently stumped, Jonathan pondered the three forks by his plate. The formally set table looked odd with plastic silverware, Jeri thought, but cleanup later should be easy.

The seating etiquette seemed pointless to her too. Jeri had to jump back up immediately to help carry in the salads and warm garlic breadsticks. A few minutes later, Jeri whispered, "Abby, sit down and eat." But Abby kept running back and forth to the kitchen, refilling glasses of sweet tea and checking the oven.

Once Emily's glass got knocked over, and Abby jumped up, but Dallas waved her back down. "We've got it," he said, grabbing his napkin. "It's just water."

Conversation felt unnatural and phony until Ms. Carter finished taking photos and left. Then Jeri sensed everyone relaxing. Her own back ached from sitting up so straight, and she slumped in relief. Conversation flowed freely then, although there was a lot more laughing at Dallas' table than theirs.

Jonathan was intent on eating his own meal—two helpings of each dish plus anything the girls couldn't finish. Between bites he asked each girl the same two questions: "Where are you from?" and "Do you have any brothers or sisters?" Jeri shook her head. He must have memorized them from some old etiquette book. Couldn't he dry up so she could hear the conversation at Dallas's table?

Jeri caught snatches of talk about the science fair the following week. She glanced behind her, green with envy at Dallas listening so intently to Emily. She was describing "interactive brain teasers to demonstrate how parts of the brain functioned." Whatever *that* meant!

"She has a good chance of winning," Brooke added. "Ms. Todd said so."

"Impressing the science teacher is one thing," Emily said. "Demonstrating for the judges is something else." She blushed then. "Anyway, Brooke's entry is just as good as mine. She's doing hers on making flowers bloom longer."

Brooke shrugged. "My parents own a florist shop. I grew up watching them arrange flowers."

Jonathan quizzed Abby about her brothers and sisters, drowning out further comments about the science fair. Jeri knew that the winner would walk away with a blue ribbon and a huge scholarship. Abby was competing in it too, with something about the food pyramid.

The month of May was filled with final competitions for scholarships: Abby in the science fair, Rosa's scrapbooking project for the art fair, Nikki's equestrian contest, and the media fair Jeri would compete in. She planned to enter her self-published sixth-grade newspaper.

The newspaper had started as a group assignment early in the school year for herself, Rosa, Abby, and Nikki. It had been an instant hit with their friends—especially Rosa's advice column—so Jeri had decided to keep publishing it. To win at the media fair, all she needed was a zinger of a front-page article. Time was getting short to find something catchy to write about.

Finally Abby stood up. "Ready for birthday cake, Emily?"

"Sure!" Emily was the kind of plain, brainy girl you barely noticed, Jeri thought, but tonight she was almost radiant.

"Everybody stay put," Abby said. "I'll be right back."

Jeri pulled the study room's heavy drapes closed to make it really dark, and then she stood by the door. A moment later, Abby called, "Lights out!" Jeri flipped the light switch and then hurried to her seat.

Abby carried in the two-layer birthday cake with twelve blazing candles. Her face shone eerily above the candlelight. "Happy birthday to you!" she sang, and everyone joined in. Dallas laughed when Emily blew too hard on the candles, spraying bits of melted wax across the cake.

Within fifteen minutes the entire cake was gone. Both boys ate two pieces. Emily escaped up to her room with the remaining chunk of cake, saving it for a midnight snack. Then the boys' ride back to Patterson arrived, and Abby walked Dallas and Jonathan to the door, thanking them for their help.

After they left, Abby closed the door and collapsed against it. "I'm bloomin' tired," she said. "Hurray for paper plates."

"I'll help clean up," Jeri said. "You did an awesome job, Abby."

"An *A* is definitely in the bag," Rosa agreed.

Abby and Jeri joked around as they washed and dried the cooking and baking dishes. Nikki and Rosa slumped in the breakfast nook, where Rosa flipped on the portable TV. When Jeri wiped off the table, she was surprised to see Nikki so pale.

"You okay?" she asked.

"Not really." Nikki's skin was an odd shade of green.

Jeri frowned. Actually, she was feeling a bit queasy herself.

Standing, Nikki grabbed the edge of the table. "I'm going to bed." She started toward the hallway. "Oh, *man*." She turned abruptly and stumbled into the small half-bath off the kitchen. She slammed the door shut and threw up, over and over. Jeri's stomach lurched at the retching sounds.

"I'll get Ms. Carter," Rosa said. She raced up the stairs to find the house mother.

Jeri knocked on the closed door. "Nikki, can I help?"

"No," she answered weakly. "I'll be okay."

Jeri looked over her shoulder at Abby. "Are you sick too?"

"No, but I didn't eat that much. Nikki had two big helpings of everything."

Jeri frowned. *I didn't eat that much either.* But if Nikki didn't stop throwing up, the retching threatened to make Jeri vomit too.

Rosa and Ms. Carter rushed into the kitchen. The house mother knocked on the bathroom door. "I'm coming in, Nikki," she said, going in and closing the door.

Jeri, Rosa, and Abby waited in the kitchen. Abby wrung her hands. "Poor Nikki! Do you think there was something wrong with what I cooked?"

"Probably," Rosa said. "Emily and Brooke are sick upstairs too, but not this bad."

Jeri's stomach cramped suddenly. "It's not your fault. Maybe the tuna was old or something. It'll be okay."

It took Nikki forever to stop throwing up. When she finally spoke, her words to the house mother were clear, even through the closed bathroom door.

"Ms. Carter," she moaned, "I think I'm going to die."

2

poisoning

Jeri gasped. Nikki *did* sound like she might die. Her weak voice was a far cry from her usual strong, bossy tone. The bathroom door opened, and Jeri and the others stepped back. Ms. Carter supported Nikki with one arm around her waist.

"I hate throwing up," Nikki muttered.

"Most people do," the house mother agreed.

"Once I get started, I can't seem to stop," Nikki said, an edge of panic in her voice. "I've always been that way."

"Really?" Ms. Carter frowned. "What usually happens?"

"I get dehydrated, and then I get shots to stop it." Nikki turned suddenly and stumbled back to the bathroom. She was sick again, but soon it sounded like her stomach was empty. *Dry heaves*, Jeri remembered her mom calling them.

Jeri's stomach rolled then, and she felt sweat beads on her upper lip. *Oh no, not me too.*

Ms. Carter ran to help Nikki. "Jeri, grab the small wastebasket from my office," the house mother called. "We may need it on the way."

"On the way to where?" Jeri asked.

"To the infirmary. I'm taking her now. If she has a history of this, there's no point in waiting until she's dehydrated." Jeri ran for the little trash can and handed it to the house mother.

Abby's face was so pale that her eyes looked like enormous coals. "This is my fault," she whispered. "It must be the food I fixed, especially if Brooke and Emily are sick too."

"They aren't *real* bad," Rosa said. "Not as bad as Nikki anyway. I'll go see if they need anything."

Jeri patted Abby's arm, willing her own stomach to stop rolling. Abby felt bad enough without her getting sick too. A moment later Ms. Carter emerged from the bathroom again, holding a weak Nikki upright. "Come on, hon. Lean on me." She helped her to a chair underneath the phone and placed the wastebasket beside her. "Use this if you have to."

Abby's voice was faint. "Can I help?"

"Yes, you both can. Abby, you keep an eye on Nikki while I check on Brooke and Emily and get my car keys." She nodded at the list of numbers posted over the phone. "Jeri, you call the Patterson School for Boys. I need to know if Dallas and Jonathan are sick too." She hurried off upstairs.

Fighting her rolling stomach, Jeri dialed the boys' school. She explained what she needed to know, then waited on hold. When the headmaster came on the line, he assured her that the boys were fine—at least, so far. "Thank you for alerting us," he said. "Tell Ms. Carter I'll be in touch if they get sick."

Jeri hung up, relieved.

Nikki sat hunched over the wastebasket, her hair hanging over her face. Jeri fished an elastic band from her pocket and loosely braided Nikki's hair to get it away from her mouth—just in case. Thirty seconds later, she was sick again.

Abby handed her some tissues when she finished. Jeri's own stomach lurched as she went to rinse out the wastebasket. If only she could keep from throwing up! Bitter-tasting bile rose in the back of her throat, and she swallowed convulsively. *Please, God, not me too!*

Ms. Carter returned then, a purse over her shoulder. "Let's go, Nikki. And don't worry, girls. The infirmary has good people on staff."

"Oh, the headmaster said Dallas and Jonathan are fine," Jeri said.

"Good. I'll call Miss Barbara from the infirmary. I'm so glad we have a doctor and nurses on the campus." Ms. Carter pressed her lips together. "I think Brooke and Emily are done being sick, and Rosa will sit with them till we get back."

Tears rolled silently down Abby's cheeks. "It's all my fault!" she said. "It has to be."

"Oh, honey, don't," Ms. Carter said, wrapping her arms around Abby. "It's *not* your fault. If the food was tainted, it was an accident. For all we know, there's a fast-acting virus going around. The doctor may be able to tell us." She peeked in the refrigerator. "Just in case, put the leftovers in a plastic bag and throw them in the garbage can outside."

"Okay."

Ms. Carter helped Nikki to her feet. Nikki's eyes glazed over as she leaned on the short house mother. "I'll call you girls when there's news," Ms. Carter said.

Jeri turned to Abby. The tiny British girl who had so happily carried in the blazing birthday cake two hours ago stared with frightened eyes. "It'll be okay," Jeri said. "Try not to worry." *Please, God, let Nikki be all right*, she prayed. A wave of heat rose up her face. *And don't let me get sick. Please!*

Abby wiped her eyes and blew her nose. "I think Ms. Carter's just being nice," she said. "My cooking must have made everyone sick. But how?"

Rosa came in then. "Maybe you didn't cook the meat enough," she answered.

Abby frowned. "I was upstairs changing when you ate the little meatballs. Did they taste funny?"

"No," Jeri said firmly, glaring at Rosa behind Abby's back. "They tasted great. Rosa ate a ton of them, and *she's* not sick."

"I didn't eat a *ton!*" Rosa protested. "But, yes, I ate four or five, and I'm fine. Maybe it's something else. Once my mom's potato salad made everyone sick at a picnic because the mayonnaise got too warm. Maybe the cream cheese in the tortilla swirls was rotten."

"Or maybe it's a *virus,* like Ms. Carter said," Jeri repeated, aggravated at Rosa. Couldn't she see how bad Abby already felt?

"If it's a virus, it came and went fast," Rosa said. "Brooke and Emily felt better as soon as they threw up a couple times."

"Okay, okay." Jeri swallowed convulsively. "Could you talk about something besides throwing up?"

"Sorry. How about a game while we wait?" Rosa suggested. "Cranium? Cards? Maybe Outburst?"

After Abby tossed out the leftovers, she and Jeri followed Rosa into the study room, and they pulled two games from the shelf. Suddenly Jeri's throat felt constricted, and she couldn't swallow. Heat rose in waves from her chest to her neck and face. "I'll be right back," she said. "I ... want to change into pj's."

Abby raised an eyebrow, but Jeri forced herself to smile as she left the room. Once out of view, she took the stairs two at a time and bolted down the hall to the restroom. She barely made it to a stall before losing every bit of food she'd eaten at the party. Jeri thought the retching would never end. Finally the spasms in her throat lessened, and her stomach settled down.

She sat back on her heels, wiped her sweaty face with a wad of toilet paper, and hauled herself to her feet. At a sink, she dampened a paper towel and washed her blotchy skin. By the time she changed her clothes and rejoined Abby and Rosa, her flushed face had returned to its normal color. *Good,* she thought. *Abby will never know.*

Thirty minutes later, Miss Barbara returned with the rest of the sixth graders who lived in Hampton House. Abby jumped up immediately and asked if any of the girls had been sick that evening.

"No. Not a soul." Miss Barbara flowed into the room, her billowing caftan making her look elegant in spite of her size. "Ms. Carter called the bowling alley and told me what happened."

Three girls pulled up chairs to watch the Cranium game in progress, and the noise level rose. "Let's wait for news in my room," Jeri said, giving up her spot in the game.

"Good idea." Abby led the way upstairs. "What if Nikki has to stay in the infirmary?" she asked. "What if she's too weak to compete next Saturday?"

"The show's still a long ways off. Don't worry yet."

The year's biggest equestrian competition was next Saturday afternoon, a week away. Nikki had brought her thoroughbred, Show Stopper, to school with her, and they competed in all kinds of horse shows. If Ms. Carter would let her, Nikki would gladly live in the barn.

At 9:30, the phone rang, and Jeri grabbed it on the first ring. Ms. Carter said Nikki was finally better—after getting three different shots to stop the vomiting. Because she was slightly dehydrated, the doctor was keeping her overnight and giving her fluids by IV. "There wasn't enough left in Nikki's stomach contents to test, but the nurse suggested food poisoning," she said.

Jeri pressed her lips together. *Food poisoning* sounded horrible. She wished she could skip that part of the message to Abby.

When she hung up, Jeri relayed the message, saying "spoiled food" instead. When they finally went to bed, Jeri curled into a ball, pressing her hand against her sore stomach. *Thank you, God.* She was grateful to feel better, but the word resounded in her brain: *poisoning.*

On Sunday morning Jeri was still sleeping hard when her alarm buzzed. Shuffling down the hall to the shower, she passed Emily and Brooke's room. The door was ajar, and she knocked. No one answered, but her light tap pushed the door open.

Their room was bright from the double windows facing east. Jeri stared in surprise at a lumpy sculpture beneath the window. The surface of the gray clay was covered with meandering red and blue lines. Those were veins, Jeri finally realized, on a brain! It must be part of Emily's science fair display. Beside the sculpture, a big red poster with giant blue letters read "BRAIN FUNCTION: Facts and Fun!" Smaller blue letters read "Puzzles and Brain Teasers Develop Reasoning Skills in Your Prefrontal Cortex!" *Whatever that means,* thought Jeri.

Another poster—yellow this time—had bold green lettering: "Can Science Improve on Mother Nature?" Nearby, jars labeled Carnations, Irises, Daffodils, and Lilies lined the windowsill. Some of the blooms looked fresh, others rather wilted. According to the poster, Brooke was testing what to add to the water—like sugar or salt—to make bouquets last longer.

Jeri hated science and was thankful not to be in the science fair. She excelled in English, though, and hoped to win the media fair award. She really needed that scholarship so she could return in the fall. Early in the school year, all Jeri had wanted to do was go back to Iowa. Now, after a year at Landmark School for Girls in Virginia, she couldn't imagine life without Abby and Rosa.

Jeri zipped through her shower in record time, glad she'd picked out her outfit the night before. She planned to wear black pants and a soft orange top that was fuzzy as a blanket. It looked good with her dark brown hair.

But when she stepped into their room and saw the pink blouse and miniskirt Rosa was wearing, it made her own outfit look babyish. She sighed inwardly. She was kidding herself. Boys weren't blind. Even someone as nice as Dallas would never notice her with Rosa around.

3

storm warning

When Jeri, Rosa, and Abby left for the church twenty minutes later, they passed Emily and Brooke coming up the stairs.

"Cool shirt, Rosa!" Brooke cried.

Jeri waited at the bottom of the stairs while Rosa told Brooke where she could buy a shirt like it. "Want me to show you?" Rosa asked. "I'm good at shopping online."

"Not today," Brooke said. "I'm saving my money for something else."

"Rosa, come *on*," Jeri said. "We'll miss the van."

They dodged light raindrops on the way to the pickup area, where the sprinkles turned to showers. They crawled into the air-conditioned van. Jeri shivered, her damp shirt clammy in the blasting air conditioning. *I hope it's warmer in church,* she thought. It wasn't. And Dallas and Jonathan weren't there, which was even more troubling.

"Where're the guys?" Rosa asked. "Their school van's here."

"I don't know." Jeri chewed her lower lip. Was Dallas back in his dorm sick? She caught her breath. Or in the *hospital*? Maybe the spoiled food hadn't hit him till later.

When they returned from church, Ms. Carter informed them that Nikki had come home that morning. They raced upstairs to find her propped up in bed, watching a movie on her laptop. *Bet it's a horse movie,* Jeri guessed. She smiled when she spotted *The Dreamer* DVD case.

"How *are* you?" Abby called, rushing across the room.

"Not bad considering my roommate tried to poison me."

At Abby's horrified expression, Jeri added, "Nikki's just kidding!"

"Says who?" Nikki paused her movie and rearranged the heating pad on her abdomen. "My stomach feels like it got ripped in half. My rear end is bruised from three shots powerful enough to stop a rhino. Riding will hurt all week."

Abby's voice was small and faint. "I'm so sorry."

"It was an accident, so give Abby a break," Jeri said. "Is there anything we can do to help?"

"Like what?" Nikki—usually the picture of indifference—had a wild look in her eyes now. "Ms. Carter won't let me go outside—doctor's orders. Do you *know* what this does to Show Stopper's exercise schedule? He needs to be worked every day! Ridden, jumped!"

"I can ride him for you," Jeri said, "but I can't jump."

"The competition's only six days away! I can't take two or three days off. It would set us back too much."

Abby stepped forward then. "This is my fault." She paused. "I'll do it for you."

"*You?*" Nikki laughed scornfully. "You're scared to death of horses."

"I can do it afraid." Abby's forced smile couldn't hide her trembling lip.

"How about this instead?" Jeri asked. "Dallas comes from a cattle ranch in Texas, and he knows horses as well as you do. I'll email him. Maybe he could exercise Show Stopper for you after school a couple days."

"Show Stopper's not a broken-down pony for some cowboy to dig his spurs into! He's a thoroughbred!"

"Look, what other choice do you have?" Jeri tried to keep the annoyance out of her voice. "I really think Dallas would take good care of your horse."

"If he's not sick too," Rosa said. "He wasn't in Sunday school today."

"Want me to go email him?" Jeri said.

Nikki scowled, staring at her motionless movie screen, and then nodded. "That might work." She cleared her throat and glanced at Abby. "Sorry I yelled at ya."

"It's okay."

Jeri left them watching the movie. She decided to instant message Dallas, in case he was already online.

Jerichogirl: HEY RU SIC?

About ten seconds later, a message appeared.

TexMex: HEY NOT NOW

Jerichogirl: NIKKI 2 INFIRMARY. HOME NOW & CRABBY

TexMex: Y

Jerichogirl: NO-1 2 EXERCISE SHOW STOPPER ON JUMPS

TexMex: FYI I KNOW HORSES. I CAN DO IT

Jerichogirl: TOMORROW?

TexMex: 2DAY IF I CAN GET RIDE W/ JAMES. HIS GF GOES 2UR SCHOOL

Jerichogirl: K

Nearly a minute passed while Jeri watched her blinking cursor. Then words popped up again.

TexMex: SORRY NOT GOING 2DAY. WHAT NOW?

Jerichogirl: IDK I CAN RIDE NOT JUMP

TexMex: IBRB

Jeri waited, but he *wasn't* right back. It was blank so long she wondered if her Internet connection was broken. Too bad his friend James wasn't coming to see his girlfriend today. Jeri was ready to close down when another message popped up.

TexMex: U THERE

Jerichogirl: AAK

TexMex: JAMES CHANGED MIND. I CAN B THERE @ 4 2 RIDE

Jerichogirl: THX NIKKI WILL B GLAD!!!!! ME2 BFN

TexMex: CU@ 4.

Jerichogirl: TTFN HAGD

HAGD. Have a great day. Jeri smiled. She planned to have a great day now too.

After a roast-and-potatoes Sunday dinner in the dining hall, Jeri changed into old clothes to wear to the barn later. They were last year's jeans, which she'd outgrown, making them fashionably tight hip huggers now. Except they didn't stay up as well as they used to, she thought, giving them an extra tug. She *wasn't* wearing tight jeans because Dallas was coming, she assured herself. They were just old, and it wouldn't matter if they got dirty. Her T-shirt covered everything as long as she kept her arms down.

Abby joined Jeri and Rosa in their room later. "Nikki's having a little kip. I'm awfully glad Dallas can help," she said. "This is all my fault."

"I'd feel rotten if I were you too," Rosa agreed.

Jeri frowned. Couldn't Rosa sound more sympathetic? Jeri tipped her desk chair back against the wall. "I bet the food from the store was bad. It was delivered, right?"

Abby nodded. "That redhead—Scottie?—brought the food."

"He's a cutie," Rosa said, smacking her lips loudly.

Jeri ignored her. "What time did he come?"

"Around three. Maybe later."

"Did you save the receipt? Something you signed?"

Abby nodded. "I had to keep records of the costs for my project."

"Can I see it?" An idea was forming in Jeri's mind. "What if—" She cut herself off. No use getting Abby's hopes up yet.

Abby retrieved the receipt, and Jeri studied it in silence. The time stamped on the signed ticket was 3:09 p.m. the day before. The store's phone number was printed at the bottom. She wondered when Scottie actually left the store with Abby's delivery. She reached for her phone. Five minutes later, she hung up and turned to Abby with a smile.

"I think I know what happened, and it *wasn't* your fault." She waved the receipt. "It says here that Scottie delivered your food at 3:09. According to Mr. Howard, he left the store before 2:00 with only one delivery—yours. The grocery store's only a ten-minute drive away, so he was probably at Landmark School by 2:10. Apparently Scottie got in trouble for taking a detour to visit his girlfriend. He must have done it before coming here." She paused and leaned forward. "Get it?"

Abby's eyes widened. "Scottie left my groceries in a hot car for an hour!"

Jeri nodded. "That's how the cold stuff spoiled."

Rosa snapped her fingers. "And why those biscuits exploded so easily. They were already hot."

"Smashing!" Abby cried, sinking back in her chair. "Brilliant."

"Let's go tell Ms. Carter," Jeri said.

"I agree with your deductions, girls," Ms. Carter said a few minutes later in her office. She hugged Abby. "Now you can stop feeling so bad. There's no way we could have known Scottie left the food in a hot car." A small frown puckered her forehead. "I *do* need to call Headmistress Long about this though. The school buys fresh produce and milk from the store. We can't have this happening again."

Jeri tapped the list. "Abby, it says you ordered fresh mushrooms."

"For the salad."

"Aren't some kinds of mushrooms poisonous?"

Ms. Carter nodded. "Yes, but not the kind you buy in the store. This time of year people get sick from eating mushrooms they find growing in the wild. Morel mushroom hunting is very popular in the spring, but people accidentally pick poisonous mushrooms as well."

An idea was forming in Jeri's mind about doing an article on accidental food poisoning for her media fair entry. She'd start her article with Nikki going to the infirmary and tell about tracking down the source of the food poisoning. Could she mention Scottie or Howard's Grocery without getting sued? Surely she'd be safe if she stuck to the truth about him leaving the food in a hot car. After all, truth was what investigative reporters uncovered and exposed.

She could also discuss other kinds of food poisoning. There must be photos online comparing poisonous and safe mushrooms. The school also had a greenhouse near the Sports Center, and she knew Mr. Petrie, the gardener.

She'd liked him ever since he gave her some flowers for Abby when she was sick a few months ago. Jeri bet she could get an interview with him and also with Nikki. Nothing like quotes from an expert plus the victim to give her article a boost.

The doorbell rang, interrupting her planning. Jeri glanced up. Four o'clock already! This time she beat Rosa to the door—barely—tugging her tight jeans higher as she walked.

Together they led Dallas back to Ms. Carter's office, and Jeri explained why he was there. "Can Nikki show Dallas what exercises to do with Show Stopper?"

"She can't go to the barn—not today. Doctor's orders." Ms. Carter tapped a pencil on the desk. "The horse show means so much to her, though. How about if she comes downstairs and gives you some instructions? Would that be enough, Dallas?"

"Yes, ma'am." He twisted his Stetson around in his hands. "I only need a list of the exercises to put him through. Jeri can show me his stall then. My ride doesn't go back to Patterson till six o'clock."

"You're kind to help her out," Ms. Carter said. "She'll be very grateful." She grinned suddenly. "Even if she doesn't show it much."

Jeri laughed and then went to get Nikki. Nikki hurried downstairs, still wearing her sweats and a wrinkled T-shirt that declared "Treat a woman like a racehorse, and she'll never be a nag." She hadn't combed her hair in two days, Jeri bet. She envied Nikki for not caring how she looked—her rumpled appearance, her bedhead, her dark sunken eyes, the sleep crease across her cheek. Show Stopper was her only concern.

Nikki wrote out a detailed list of exercises, giving Dallas all kinds of pointers that Jeri knew he didn't need. But Dallas just nodded. Then she produced a digital camera for Jeri. "Photograph each exercise from every angle. Also try to snap the exact moment they go over fences."

Jeri nodded and slipped the camera case strap over her shoulder. "Let's go," she said, smiling at Dallas.

"Wait up!"

Jeri turned as Rosa grabbed her pink ball cap from the hall tree. Jeri fumed silently. Why did Rosa have to come? She'd do all the talking now.

Nikki disappeared into the study while Jeri waited for Rosa to make a ponytail. From inside the study, Jeri heard Brooke ask Nikki for a small loan. "Just for a couple days till Dad puts my allowance in my account."

"Okay," Nikki said, "but no more till you pay me back."

Jeri shook her head. She couldn't imagine being Nikki or Brooke, whose parents filled their checking accounts. *Oh, well!* "Come on, Rosa. Your hair looks fine."

Rosa followed them out the door and pulled it closed after her. "Thanks for helping Nikki," Rosa said, falling into step on the other side of Dallas.

Jeri moved over to make room for her on the narrow sidewalk and slipped off the edge, turning her ankle. She could walk in the grass beside Dallas, but that felt stupid. Jeri dropped behind them. Dallas glanced over his shoulder, moved to the grass himself, and motioned Jeri forward to walk in the middle. Her heart warmed as she moved between them. Rosa didn't seem to care, though, as she chattered nonstop all the way to the barn.

The next two hours was the most fun Jeri'd had in weeks. She could have watched Dallas trot and canter around the outdoor ring all night. He barely touched the saddle, not *thwumping* it repeatedly like some of the riders. Jeri noticed several girls studying Dallas on Nikki's thoroughbred.

As Jeri photographed Dallas, she couldn't help wishing she'd worn a bigger pair of jeans. She had to stretch to take the photos, and every time she reached up to snap a picture, she felt a breeze on her bare stomach. At least Dallas was too busy to watch her.

Jeri's heart leapt as Dallas and Show Stopper sailed over one barrier and hedge after another. If she didn't know better, she'd guess Dallas had been riding Show Stopper for years instead of an hour. Nikki could relax. Her horse was in good hands.

Rosa climbed on the bottom fence board beside her and hung her arms over the top. "Getting some good pictures?"

"I think so." Jeri shaded her eyes against the setting sun.

"Do you like Dallas?" Rosa asked. "I could help you get him." She gave Jeri's outfit a once-over. "It wouldn't be that hard if you dressed like that every day."

"I don't want to *get* him!" Jeri concentrated on taking more photos, glad for an excuse not to look at Rosa, but she felt the heat crawling up her neck.

"Playing hard to get?" Rosa wrinkled her nose. "That's not my style, but it might work on Dallas."

"Oh stop it, Rosa," Jeri said. "Dallas is friends with me, like he is with every girl."

"It wouldn't have to stay that way." When Jeri didn't respond, Rosa shrugged. "Suit yourself. See ya later." Rosa wandered over to a group of girls.

Jeri watched her go and then turned to take more pictures. Across the exercise ring, several small groups of people had lined up along the fence to watch. Jeri ignored them and kept taking pictures until Dallas finished the last exercise.

Later, while Dallas brushed Show Stopper's glistening coat, Jeri carried buckets of water to the stall. In the corner by the hay bag, she noticed a dark cloth and bent to get it. It was a blue bandana. "Is this yours?"

"Nope." Dallas pulled one from his back pocket. "Mine's right here."

Jeri hung the dusty bandana over the stall door and then got an apple from the bucket that Sam, the stable hand, always left by the tack room.

"Here." She handed it to Dallas.

"Thanks." He glanced at her stomach, then away. "Show Stopper earned it."

"So did you!" Self-consciously, Jeri tugged her shirt

down. "Nikki was so worried earlier today. Thank you for doing this."

Dallas grinned. "I enjoyed it. We can't afford to board my horse at school, so this has been fun for me."

"I know Nikki's grateful too."

Suddenly tongue-tied, she turned quickly and bent to brush dust from her jeans. She liked being Dallas's friend, but she'd lied to Rosa earlier. She *didn't* want to just be friends with him. But would a boy as nice as Dallas Chandler ever notice a girl as uncool as Jeri McKane?

She let out a big sigh. Talk about wishful thinking.

4

danger, warning, caution

Monday after school Nikki was waiting for Jeri when she got back to the dorm. Under her wild and uncombed hair, her face was a mottled red, but Jeri couldn't tell if she was sick again—or mad.

"What's wrong?" she asked, hanging her jacket on the hall tree.

"Your friend Dallas is a dumb cowboy!" she snapped. "Show Stopper's sick today. Sam called from the horse barn."

"Sick?" Jeri frowned. "A fever? What?"

"He won't eat! Dallas must have fed him the wrong food! I bet he didn't cool him down after his workout either."

"He did just what you told him to," Jeri said. Nikki had a lot of nerve, even if she *was* worried.

"Well, Show Stopper's totally off his feed and really sluggish. Why?"

"I don't know. Maybe Sam should call the vet."

"He did." Nikki plopped down on the bottom step of the staircase. "He couldn't find anything wrong."

Jeri sat beside her. "Show Stopper probably just misses *you* as much as you miss him," she said.

"You think so?" Nikki gave a lopsided grin. "Maybe you're right. Sorry."

Jeri grinned back.

Late that night Jeri read her murder mystery in bed long after Rosa fell asleep. At the end of her chapter, her bedside clock read 11:21. She yawned so wide her jaws popped. If she didn't get to sleep soon, she'd snooze through her classes tomorrow.

She headed to the restroom, her feet padding quietly in the empty hall. She'd finished and was washing her hands when she heard running footsteps. Brooke pushed open the restroom door and dashed to a stall. She was sick to her stomach once, then again.

And again.

The toilet flushed, but Brooke didn't come out. Jeri finally swung open the stall door. Overhead lights were bright, shining down on Brooke where she sat on the tile floor, eyes closed.

Jeri knelt beside her. "Are you okay?"

"I'm fine." Brooke clutched her stomach. "*Now* anyway."

Jeri felt Brooke's forehead like her mom always did when Jeri had the flu. "You don't feel feverish."

"I think it was something I ate. I got hungry while I was doing homework, so I went downstairs for a piece of cold pizza." She wrinkled her nose. "It didn't stay down."

"Was the pizza yours?" Each girl had her own small cupboard and a small labeled plastic container in the huge fridge for their own special food.

"Yeah, it was mine." Brooke stared at Jeri. "Why?"

"Nothing." Jeri took Brooke's arm and helped her to her feet. "What's that?" she asked, pointing to a rash on her hands. "Maybe you have chicken pox or measles."

"I don't. It's allergies, that's all."

"Can you make it back to your room alone? I'll go get Ms. Carter."

"*No.* Don't do that." Brooke leaned against the wall.

"But what if it's not allergies? Let Ms. Carter make sure you're okay."

"No. She'll make a big deal out of nothing. I don't want her hauling me off to the infirmary like she did Nikki. I've got too much to do before the science fair on Friday."

"You might need some medicine. Otherwise, you could be so sick by Friday that you'd *still* miss the science fair."

"I won't be. I *won't.*"

Jeri rubbed the back of her neck. What was wrong with Brooke? "All right. I hope you feel better."

One bedroom door opened down the hall, and then another one. "What's going on out here?"

"Quiet out there! Some people are trying to sleep!"

"Sorry," Brooke said.

"You couldn't help it," Jeri said, then raised her voice. "She's sick!"

"I'm okay now." Brooke headed back to her room. "I feel better already."

When Jeri returned to bed, she couldn't settle down to sleep. This was the second time in two days someone got sick from food fixed in the dorm kitchen. What was going on? They couldn't blame the delivery boy *this* time. Something about Brooke's insistence on keeping her illness a secret seemed strange. Was she really protecting herself from Ms. Carter's mothering? Something didn't add up. Whatever it was, Jeri was thoroughly awake now.

Tiptoeing past her sleeping roommate, Jeri turned the bright computer screen away from Rosa and then Googled "food poisoning." She could use the information for her newspaper—and maybe discover what was happening in the dorm at the same time.

But forty minutes later when she logged off, Jeri hadn't found anything helpful. The next morning she told Rosa about Brooke's episode in the restroom. "I've decided not to eat any food from the dorm kitchen from now on."

"Oh, that's crazy," Rosa said. "Brooke probably ate half a pizza instead of one piece and made herself sick from pigging out."

"Maybe," Jeri admitted, remembering the rash and Brooke's odd behavior. *Or maybe not.*

Once a week, the house mothers fixed a lip-smacking breakfast for any girl who wanted to eat in the dorm. Usually Jeri loved trooping downstairs in her pajamas to eat waffles or pancakes, but this Tuesday morning the aroma wafting up the stairs didn't tempt her.

"I'm eating at the dining hall," Jeri reminded Rosa. "You coming?"

"Are you nuts? I smell fresh coffee cake and banana bread!"

"Don't get sick then," Jeri warned. "I'm not taking any chances."

"Talk about paranoid," Rosa said, pulling on her bunny slippers.

Ten minutes later in the noisy dining hall, after gobbling down some Frosted Flakes, Jeri headed to the greenhouse to interview Mr. Petrie. A gentle breeze blew as she strolled along sidewalks bordered by terra-cotta pots of impatiens and petunias. The carillon bells in the tower chimed as she skirted around a stand of white pine. The horse barn was on her far left, and then she passed the Sports Center. Lawn mowers zigzagged over the soccer field, and several high school girls jogged around the track. Jeri veered off the sidewalk and followed a white-rock path to the greenhouse.

The outside reminded Jeri of a gardening store, with its bags of rock, mulch, and fertilizer stacked beside clay pots, shovels, and three wheelbarrows. She meandered through everything to step inside the huge shed-like room attached to the greenhouse. At first, the darkness blinded her, so she stopped a minute and breathed deeply the smells of wet dirt and mulch. Where did she know that smell from? For some reason, it put her right back in Iowa on her grandpa's farm.

"Hello?" Jeri called, peering around the dim room. No answer. Mr. Petrie must be out in the greenhouse part where he grew the plants.

A scurrying noise to her left made her whirl around. She peered into the shadows. Was it mice? She shuddered. Or *rats*? A shadow darted from behind a clay pot, and tiny claws scritch-scratched across the cement floor. Jeri pivoted to run.

Her elbow hit a rack of hoes and shovels, and several clattered to the cement floor. The clanging echoed and rang in her ears. She groped for the handles and stood them back up, and then worked her way to a door at the back. *Let me out of this cave!*

Beyond the door was a room full of light with walls made of glass or plastic. It was twenty degrees warmer, and Jeri unzipped her jacket. The sun pounding down on the clear roof turned the greenhouse into an oven. Sunlight shone on long rows of tables full of small potted plants. Baskets of ferns and ivy sprinkled by misters hung above her, and she felt the moisture.

She moved away and called again. "Anybody here? Hello?"

Mr. Petrie must be outside. Jeri started down an aisle of potted flowers she recognized from home: pansies, bachelor's buttons, and marigolds. No wonder all the flower beds on campus were so colorful. The next aisle over contained vegetables she and her mom used to grow, like tomato plants and green peppers. She guessed the viney plants like cucumbers and melons were outside. The greenhouse grew more of the school's food than she'd thought.

Jeri glanced at her watch. If only Mr. Petrie were here. A good quote for her article was all she needed before heading to her first-period library class to write it up.

She strolled up the last aisle and, without warning, stubbed her toe hard on something under the table. Jeri sucked in her breath and bent to see what she'd kicked.

Underneath were various bags and boxes of plant food, insecticide for garden pests, and weed killers. No wonder Mr. Petrie's plants looked like blue-ribbon winners at a county fair, Jeri thought, if he put all that stuff on them.

On a box of weed killer, the word *Warning!* caught her eye. She crouched down and read: *Children are highly sensitive to the harmful effects of pesticides. Exposure to pesticides may produce brain cancer, leukemia, and birth defects.*

Whoa! This stuff was deadly. Why wasn't it locked up somewhere? What if a person got it on his hands and then touched his food? Was it possible that—

"What in blue blazes are you doing there?" thundered a deep voice from behind her. "How many times do I have to tell you kids—"

Jeri jerked, falling over backward and cracking her elbow on the cement floor. She dropped and spilled the box of weed killer. "I ... uh ... I ..."

"I repeat, what are you doing?" Mr. Petrie asked.

"I was looking for you, actually." Jeri crawled to her feet and turned to face him. "Hi, Mr. Petrie," she said sheepishly, wishing she'd had a chance to clean up the mess before he saw it. And yet, she didn't really want to touch poisonous stuff.

Mr. Petrie's bushy gray eyebrows shot up. "I didn't recognize you. I was fixin' to chew you out." His grass-stained fingers clenched a spade balanced on the toe of one worn work boot.

Jeri wrinkled her nose at the acrid smell of the pesticide. "If you'll show me where you keep your broom, I'll clean that up."

"Nah, I'll get it. I don't want you touchin' that stuff. It's dangerous."

"Yeah, I saw the label."

"Good eyes." Mr. Petrie nudged the box with his toe. "Always read labels."

"Why?"

"Labels have signal words that tell how poisonous something is."

"Signal words?"

"Words like *danger,* which means very toxic or poisonous, or *warning,* which is medium poisonous. *Caution* means a little toxic." He paused. "Say, shouldn't you be in class?"

"Class is why I'm here. I wanted to interview you for an article."

"Interview *me*?" He grinned. "What for?"

"About the food you grow here, mostly, and also about, well, food poisoning."

He frowned. "Why that?"

Jeri explained about her friends being sick from something they ate, and she was writing an article on food poisoning. "I heard you grew the school's vegetables."

"You think my vegetables *poisoned* someone?"

"No, I didn't mean that." An idea occurred to her though. "Are weed killers ever missing?"

"You mean stolen? Naw. Kids don't steal from me. Usually it's only careless pranks that cause me trouble."

"Like what?"

"Nothing big—just irritating things. Science classes come through on field trips and knock over plants. Softballs break windows. Occasionally horses from the barn get loose and run through the garden. Makes my job harder than it needs to be."

Jeri dug into her backpack for a small notebook and pen. "Can I ask you a few questions?"

"Thought you just did." He grinned and moved away. "Talk to me while I water."

Jeri trotted behind him while he grabbed a rubber hose, turned a spigot, and began to water the first aisle of plants. He talked about how he started vegetables growing indoors during the cold Virginia winters and then transplanted them outside in the spring, plus how he used bumblebees inside the greenhouse for pollination.

Choosing her words carefully, Jeri steered him to the topic she was most interested in. "Do you grow mushrooms here?"

"Naw."

"I heard that people go mushroom hunting at this time of year and accidentally eat poisonous mushrooms."

"True. They can be hard to tell apart," he said. "Mushrooms aren't the only problem. Quite a few common plants are poisonous." He motioned her to follow him. Back inside the main building, Mr. Petrie led the way to a small room that turned out to be his office. A bookshelf filled one wall, and he handed her a book with a tattered cover.

"*Wild Plants of Virginia*," she read aloud. It was filled with colorful photos.

"You'll find a good bit in there about poisonous plants," he said.

"Can I borrow this?" Jeri asked. "I could bring it back in a couple days."

"Sure." He rummaged on his messy desk for a pen and paper. "Just write your name down here ... and your dorm. If you don't return it by Friday, I'll come lookin' for you." He winked.

"I'll bring it back. Thanks!" She wedged it into her backpack and zipped it shut. "Thanks, Mr. Petrie. I'd better go."

"Not till you scrub," he said, motioning to a sink in the corner of his office. "You touched that weed killer. You might put your hands in your mouth."

"I won't."

"Do it anyway. Lather up real good there," he said. "Lots of suds."

Jeri sighed. He made her sound like a baby, but she didn't have time to argue. She washed and rinsed and then wiped her dripping hands on her blue uniform jumper. "Thanks again!" She hurried out of the nursery and raced up the hill.

In library first hour, Jeri leafed through the plant book and found one alarming thing. She saw that the medicine her mom kept in their cupboard at home—ipecac syrup —was actually made from a poisonous plant! The berries and juice from that plant caused nausea and vomiting. Ipecac syrup was used to make poison victims throw up and get rid of poison quickly.

Jeri stared at the bell tower outside her window. The ipecac plant was found in all parts of the country, according to the book. Could it have somehow found its way into their food at Hampton House?

She read on about many common plants that were poisonous and easy to find. They were often accidentally used in salads and casseroles—to a deadly end. Jeri leaned back and gazed unseeingly at white clouds floating behind the bell tower.

Yes, deadly plants could be ingested accidentally. But just as easily, someone in Hampton House could be using them on purpose.

5

poison potatoes

When the bell rang, Jeri raced across campus to Herald Hall for literature class. She caught up with Rosa at the classroom door. "Where's Abby?" Jeri asked.

Rosa whipped around. "*She's* sick now! So are Emily and Miss Barbara! It happened after breakfast."

"See?" Jeri cried. "I told you not to eat the food in the kitchen. Is Nikki sick again too?"

"No, but she didn't eat. She was at the horse barn since before breakfast doing some jumping."

"How's *your* stomach?" Jeri asked, following her into class.

"Fine, and I ate what everyone else ate." Rosa shrugged. "It's a virus. It has to be."

"I don't think so. I'm even more convinced that it's poison."

"Oh come on. You're just inventing a poison plot so you can write about something exciting and win the media award."

"That's not true—or fair!" Jeri sputtered. "In a book of Mr. Petrie's I read about a bunch of common plants that can be poisonous. This is no virus. I just know it."

Jeri could tell Rosa was still skeptical, but she'd talk to Ms. Carter right after class today. She'd show her Mr. Petrie's book, and then the house mother would see that they must be using contaminated food from somewhere. They were being poisoned—either by accident or on purpose. Jeri was sure of it.

The afternoon turned hot—mid-eighties—and at 3:30 Jeri gladly changed out of her school uniform. Cut-offs and a baggy T-shirt felt perfect.

She knocked on Abby's door, but no one answered. Jeri trotted down the hall to the restroom and called Abby's name, but she wasn't there. *At least she's not sick again,* Jeri thought. *That's good.* She was probably watching TV. Carrying Mr. Petrie's book, she headed for Ms. Carter's tiny office behind the kitchen. She had to tell the house mother what she suspected.

Ms. Carter sat at her desk and listened carefully as Jeri listed reasons she believed their dorm food was being poisoned.

"But I'm the one who cooked breakfast today," Ms. Carter said. "The food was fine."

"But what if you couldn't tell? What if someone dies next time?"

Ms. Carter came around to the front of the desk and put her arms around Jeri. "I understand your fear. First Nikki goes to the infirmary and now Abby. Of course you're—"

"Abby?" Jeri pulled back. "She's in the infirmary?"

"I thought you knew." Ms. Carter leaned against the edge of her desk. "She was sick several times this morning, and I put her in the infirmary to be watched. She's so tiny and frail. I didn't want to take any chances."

"Can I go see her?" Jeri said, already heading to the door.

"I'm afraid not. The doctor disagreed with the nurse and suspects a virus. He wants to isolate any sick girls so no one else picks it up."

Jeri was unconvinced, but she could tell Ms. Carter didn't believe her poisoning theory. She trudged back upstairs, more worried about Abby than Ms. Carter knew.

She was studying the plant book when Rosa walked in. "Did you hear about Abby?" Rosa asked, tossing her books and purse on the bed.

"Yes, and we can't see her either."

"I know."

Jeri stretched. "What are you going to do now?"

"Brooke and I are taking homework outside. It's an excuse to get some sun."

Jeri raised one eyebrow. "You don't need to tan. You were born with one."

"I know." Rosa giggled and pulled on a pink tank top and gray short shorts.

"Where'd you get those?"

"Online." She turned back and forth before the mirror. "I love having clothes delivered to my door."

"Those shorts barely cover your bum. Don't bend over."

"Oh, stop being a grandma."

"I'm not!"

"If you didn't have white stick legs, you'd wear short shorts too."

That stung. "No. I wouldn't." Jeri turned back to her book, tears threatening to spill over. Even if she had a terrific tan, she wouldn't walk around half naked. She didn't see how Rosa could either.

Rosa left in silence, and Jeri buckled down to work on her entry for the media fair. She learned from Mr. Petrie's book that poisonous and safe mushrooms often grew side by side. One particular small brown poisonous mushroom often grew under white pine trees—and they had white pines all over campus! If you ate one of those mushrooms, she read, the reaction time was within an hour. It required stomach pumping and throwing up to get rid of it.

Had someone—somehow—added poisonous mushrooms to Abby's salad last Saturday night?

On the way to the greenhouse to return Mr. Petrie's book, Jeri didn't spot Rosa and Brooke, but there were about a hundred blankets spread out on the grass. School books lay on most of them, but few girls were studying. Instead they were laughing, napping, reading magazines, chatting on cell phones, and catching some rays.

Out behind the greenhouse, Mr. Petrie was dragging a hose down a row of flowers, soaking each plant for several seconds before moving on.

"Hey, Mr. Petrie!" Jeri called, waving the book. "Thanks for letting me use this. Want me to put it in your office?"

"No, just park it there." He pointed to a picnic table. "Find what ya needed?"

"I think so." She turned slowly in a circle. There was an acre or more of garden plots back here, some big and some tiny, all staked off. "Who do all these gardens belong to?"

"I grow food in the big ones for the school." He finished watering to the end of the row, pulled off a few yellowed leaves, and then turned off the water. "My stuff's bigger and fresher than Howard's produce. I dunno why the headmistress buys so much in town. I also grow flowers for the flower beds and for bouquets for dinners and banquets."

"What about those little gardens?"

"The smaller plots belong to students—mostly biology or horticultural. They planted seeds in the greenhouse in February and transplanted seedlings outdoors last month. Each plot's got a stake with a name on it."

"Mom and I grew a garden back in Iowa too. I ate a lot of sugar peas when I was supposed to be weeding." Jeri shaded her eyes. "That's rhubarb over there, isn't it? That's my mom's favorite thing to eat raw. Talk about sour!" Her lip curled.

"Did you know its dark green leaves are poisonous? Use that for your article."

"Really? What happens if you eat them?"

"Nasty stuff. Trouble breathing, burning in the mouth, vomiting." Mr. Petrie pulled weeds from a row of bushy plants behind them. "Lots of ordinary plants are poisonous, like rhubarb and mushrooms and narcissus and daffodil bulbs. And here you have potatoes. It surprises people to know that the ordinary potato can poison them."

"You're kidding! How?" Jeri asked, grabbing her notebook and writing fast.

"The poison's in the green parts of a potato that aren't ripe and the sprouts—those little 'eyes'." He knelt and pulled up an unripe potato plant, then pointed to the green parts that were poisonous. Jeri grabbed her camera from her backpack. "The poison in potatoes is called solanine," he added.

While Mr. Petrie talked, Jeri got half a dozen photos. This was just what she needed for her article. "Do you throw up if you eat the green parts?"

"Yup." He replanted the potato and stood. "You also might have a burning sensation in your throat, headaches, pain in your stomach ... maybe even death."

"Death?"

"Yes, if you ate a whole *lot* of green parts. It happens quick—fifteen to thirty minutes—before anyone figures out it was a potato causing the problem. You studyin' to be a doctor or something?"

"Last weekend some girls in my dorm got sick. I think it was food poisoning. My friend Nikki ended up in the infirmary."

"Nikki Brown?" Mr. Petrie asked.

Jeri blinked in surprise. "Yeah. How'd you know that?"

"When you checked out that book, you wrote Hampton House on the paper. Last month a girl named Nikki from that dorm let her horse get loose and trample some of the gardens. She got mad when her show horse ate some bad weeds and got sick."

"Bad weeds? Like what?"

"Dunno. He could have eaten milkweed pods or foxglove. Even Jimsonweed. Hard to say. Somehow she figured her horse eating weeds was my fault. She got real mad."

"Sounds like Nikki. She's horse crazy."

"Like half the girls here," he said, chuckling then. "Keeping her horse under control would do more good than bellyaching to the headmistress."

Jeri bit her lower lip. Had Nikki complained to the Head and gotten him in trouble? Was that what he meant? A disquieting thought occurred to her. Under his easygoing attitude, was Mr. Petrie angry at Nikki? Angry enough to want to pay her back? Surely not.

Hmmm … *Had* Show Stopper just eaten some bad weeds? Jeri remembered the stable hand saying Mr. Petrie supplied hay and apples for the horses. Her heart beat faster, and the pulse in her neck jumped. It would be simple to put apples dusted with weed poison into Show Stopper's stall or to add things like green potatoes or rhubarb leaves to the horse's mesh hay bag. Of course, she was assuming it was poisonous to animals too. Maybe not.

She tapped her notebook with her pencil. "Um, does the food that poisons people also hurt animals—small pets or even horses?"

"In big enough doses, yes. Rhubarb, green potatoes, avocadoes …" He paused in concentration. "Plus mushrooms, onions, and tomato leaves and stems bother horses."

"What usually happens? Do they throw up too?"

"No, it gives them colic—stomach cramps. Or muscle spasms and trouble swallowing. If a horse eats enough, he'll collapse."

Jeri kept her eyes on her paper. He sure knew a lot about horses for a gardener. Why? After thanking him for his help, she glanced at her watch and headed straight to the dining hall. Clouds were gathering in the west, and the breeze was cooler. Her stomach growled like an irritated bear.

But supper went right out of her mind the minute she stepped inside the dining hall. Claire James, the junior editor of the school paper the *Lightning Bolt,* slammed into her. Jeri staggered back, waiting for an apology. It didn't come.

"Watch where you're going, kid!" Claire snapped, adjusting her tiny eyeglasses.

"Sorry," Jeri muttered.

"Well, if it isn't Landmark School's hotshot reporter!" Claire laughed harshly and flung her long red hair back over her shoulder. "Did you finally get smart and give up writing?"

"No." Jeri took a deep breath. "I've been busy writing. I'm entering my sixth-grade newspaper in the media fair."

"You're joking! Like *you* could win." Her mocking tone sent a chill through Jeri.

"I might," Jeri said. And with tuition going up, she needed that full scholarship that came with first place. "I have as good a chance as anyone."

"Ya think?" Claire snorted. "I've seen some of the entries. Ms. Gludell's collecting them at the newspaper office. She's one of the judges." She leaned close to Jeri's nose. "You haven't got a prayer."

"Like you would know!" Jeri's heart pounded so hard her chest hurt. "Ms. Gludell wouldn't tell you anything."

"But I heard her talking to another teacher. Sierra Sedgewick is doing a photo essay showing the diversity of weather in Virginia. She's making a book out of the photos."

"Sierra?" Jeri's head jerked up and she pressed her lips together, now feeling both scared and mad. Sierra

Sedgewick's father owned his own photography studio in Norfolk. She remembered the last media project Sierra turned in. Rosa said her dad had done it—it was really professional. What if her media fair project—the photo essay book—was done by her father too?

I can't compete with that! Jeri thought. *God, what am I going to do?*

She pivoted on her heel and left the dining hall without another word. The media fair entry wasn't due till Monday morning. She wasn't going to worry about what she couldn't control. *Just do your best and give God the rest.* That's what her mom always said.

What could beat Sierra's photo book though? If only she had something more exciting to write about than mushrooms and rhubarb! She *had* done some investigative reporting earlier in the year—even helped the police once. Writing about something like that just might beat Sierra.

She'd lost her appetite, so she plodded to the library, her mind already trying (and discarding) several ideas she could investigate. It was already Wednesday night! No one—not even Rosa—believed the girls in Hampton House were being poisoned. But there must be something else she could write about. How could she find an idea outstanding and unique enough to investigate, solve, and write about—before Monday?

6

creepy crawlies

At the library Jeri spent an hour in a study carrel scanning newspapers and news magazines for something to investigate. There were controversies about local air pollution, a logging company cutting too many trees, and littering around Sutter Lake. All important topics—but they sounded deadly dull to Jeri.

Lightning flashed in the distance, and Jeri decided to head back to Hampton House before a storm hit. Disappointed, she pushed back her chair and hurried home, glad to beat the rain. For now, until something better came up, she'd have to stick to her article on food poisoning.

But when she walked in the front door at 7:30, something she heard drove the whole project out of her mind.

From down the hall drifted the sound of Dallas's voice! What was *he* doing here?

She peeked around the doorway into the living room. He was sprawled in a rocker, and Rosa was perched on the arm of the couch, chatting away.

"Hi, Jeri!" Dallas called when he spotted her. He sat forward. "Where ya been?"

"At the library. I'm still working on my media fair project." She leaned against the door jamb. "How long have you been here?"

"Barely a minute. I caught a ride over with my friend who's visiting his girlfriend." He turned his cowboy hat around by the brim. "I thought I'd check to see if Nikki needed help with her horse again."

"She's fine now," Jeri said. "Just tired—"

"No, she's *not* fine," Rosa interrupted. "After supper she got sick again. So did Emily and Brooke. Emily's so bad they took her to the hospital! Brooke went along with her and Miss Barbara."

"The *hospital*?"

"Emily was all bent over," Rosa said. "She could hardly walk. Brooke felt sick too, but she practically carried Emily to the car. She's worried sick."

Jeri knew she'd react the same way if Rosa was deathly sick. "Has anyone heard from them?"

"Not yet."

Dallas spoke up then. "Where'd those three girls eat supper?"

"In the dining hall."

"Anybody else who ate the meal there get sick?" he asked.

Rosa shrugged. "Not that I know of."

Hmmm, Jeri thought. That blew her food poisoning theory. "I guess you could be right then," she admitted slowly. "They didn't eat in the dorm kitchen, so those girls must have a virus that they can't shake."

"Or *not.*" Underneath Rosa's tan, her face looked pale. "We were all watching a movie and having snacks after supper—Emily, Brooke, Nikki, and me. Emily shared her trail mix with us. I'm the only one who didn't get sick."

"But you *all* ate the snacks?" Jeri asked, dropping her backpack and coming into the room.

"I didn't." Rosa turned her back to Dallas and lowered her voice. "I'm trying to lose a few pounds, so I gave my trail mix to Nikki." Her eyes clouded over. "Ms. Carter's upstairs helping her—*and* Abby. Abby came home from the infirmary at noon and is so tired." Rosa shuddered. "I'm keeping my snacks upstairs from now on. I don't care if it *is* against the rules."

"Where do you usually keep them?" Dallas asked.

"In the kitchen," Rosa said. "We each have a small cupboard shelf, and we have a plastic basket in the fridge with our name on it. Everybody's supposed to stay out of everyone else's stuff."

Dallas glanced at Jeri. "It *does* sound like someone's messing with your food."

Jeri rubbed the back of her neck. "Maybe. Maybe not. I found out in a book Mr. Petrie loaned me how many common foods we have that can be *poisonous*. Rhubarb, unripe potatoes, mushrooms, stuff like that. Plus growers use insecticides and weed killers that might still be on the fruit and vegetables. Trail mix has dried fruit in it." She paused. "Even so, three cases of food poisoning in three days is suspicious."

Dallas sat forward, a frown making a pucker between his eyebrows. "I'm not sure how to say this without making Nikki sound bad ..."

"What is it?" Jeri asked.

"Well, I like her. I really do. But I've noticed that she can be a little ... well ... loud and bossy sometimes."

"No kidding," Rosa muttered.

"Has she made an enemy in your dorm? Anyone she's insulted or anything?"

"She insults everybody!" Rosa said. "Abby probably gets it the worst, living with her."

Dallas paced around the living room. "If somebody's mad at her, knocking her out of the jumping competition would be great revenge. She said it's the biggest equestrian event of the year."

"With the biggest prize." Jeri frowned. "I'm sure people in the riding club are tired of Nikki winning all the time, but no one in our dorm cares. Nikki's the only one here competing in the equestrian contest."

Rosa nodded. "Most of the girls in the horse club are older."

Jeri snapped her fingers. "They're at the riding ring most days. When I was photographing Dallas, some kids across the ring were watching. Afterwards, when I was carrying water, several girls asked me why Dallas was riding Show Stopper."

"Maybe they're in the background of the pictures," Rosa said. "Where're the photos?"

"Upstairs. I printed off a few." Jeri's face flushed hotly. She'd printed out some of the photos of Dallas to keep for herself. Rosa grinned but said nothing.

Jeri ran upstairs for them and then spread them out on the coffee table. Together, they studied each photo.

"Hey!" Rosa said, pointing. "Isn't that Janeen Jenkins? She was in my swimming class last semester. She's on the equestrian team."

Jeri leaned closer and squinted. "Is she the eighth grader who always comes in second? I bet she'd love it if Nikki couldn't compete."

Dallas plopped back down on the couch. "But how could this eighth grader get into your dorm to poison Nikki's food?"

Rosa peered closer at the last photo and squealed. "Scottie!"

"What?" Jeri asked.

"The delivery boy! Look!" Rosa jabbed the photo with her long nail. "He was in the crowd watching too. I've seen him with Janeen before. That's who he was visiting when he was late with Abby's delivery last weekend."

Dallas leaned forward on his thighs. "The delivery boy's girlfriend is this Janeen?"

"Yes. And remember that blue bandana I found in the stall? Look here." Jeri pointed at Scottie. "There's something dark tied around his neck."

Dallas slapped his knee. "Didn't Nikki say Show Stopper wouldn't eat yesterday? Maybe Scottie tampered with the horse feed while I was jumping. It'd be easy—no one was in Show Stopper's stall for over an hour."

"Makes sense." Jeri tried to stay calm. "Rosa, are you sure his girlfriend is Janeen?"

"One way to find out." Rosa tossed her hair over her shoulder. "Give me half a minute. I'll call Shauna. She knows everything about who's dating who." Rosa ran upstairs and was back in five minutes. "Bingo. Scottie and Janeen are a couple. Now what?"

Jeri jabbed the photo. "Then he must be trying to help her win by knocking out the competition. Then Janeen wins the scholarship and comes back to Landmark next year."

At last! Things were falling into place. Nikki didn't need the scholarship money, but she was the most likely one to win. She had a string of blue ribbons taped around her mirror upstairs from previous competitions this year. Jeri could only remember one contest where Nikki and Show Stopper hadn't walked away with the top prize.

What if Janeen and Scottie were that desperate for this final win—and the scholarship?

Jeri's head was spinning. "Could Scottie *really* tamper with our dorm food so many times?" she asked. "The food for the birthday dinner would have been easy, but the left-over pizza Monday night?" She looked from Rosa to Dallas. "And even if Brooke and Emily bought the trail mix at the grocery store, could Scottie have messed with it?" She shook her head. "I don't see how. They would have noticed if the package was opened."

"But it doesn't come in sealed packages," Dallas said. "The dried pineapple and nuts and stuff are in these bins with lids. You scoop out how much you want, and then they weigh it."

"So that's when Scottie added something to the trail mix?" Rosa asked.

"That *must* be it!" Jeri shuddered involuntarily.

Rosa grabbed Jeri's hand. "Call the police. Let them handle it."

Jeri bit her lower lip. "They'd never believe me, not without some proof." *But some serious snooping on my own might provide that evidence.* If she could discover who was behind the poisonings, it might also provide the investigative report she needed to win the media fair scholarship. *God, is this what you want me to do? If it is, show me what to do.*

Just then the front door opened, and Miss Barbara and Brooke were heard in the entryway. When they passed by the living room, they were supporting Emily between them. Brooke was as pale as Emily, but Jeri couldn't tell if it was sickness or fear for her roommate.

"Emily, are you all right?" Rosa asked.

"She will be after a good night's rest," the hefty assistant house mother said. "We need to get her tucked into bed now though."

As Brooke passed, Jeri whispered, "What'd they do to her?"

"Pumped her stomach," Brooke said with a shudder, "but there wasn't anything left." They slowly climbed the stairs while the trio watched from below.

Dallas cleared his throat. "Jeri, you want to ask Nikki if she needs me to exercise Show Stopper again? I still have time before I go back."

"Sure. I'll ask." She ran upstairs and was back in a minute. "Nikki says no thanks. She practiced this morning already, before breakfast. And she'll be well enough to do it tomorrow." She grinned then. "She also invited you to come, if you can, to her competition Saturday afternoon."

"That'd be great," Dallas said. "Tell her I'll be there."

Rosa walked with him to the front door, cute as a model in her short shorts and tank top. Jeri watched and prayed, *God, forgive me for envying girls who dress for attention—and get it.* Was her mom right? Would Jeri be attractive to boys someday for her good character traits and being friendly? Jeri sure hoped so.

All during classes on Wednesday, Jeri couldn't concentrate. So much had happened since Saturday night, and her mind reeled as she tried to make sense of it. Three incidents in four days—it had to be poisoning of some kind. Was it accidental food poisoning—or was someone poisoning their food on purpose? And if so, *why?*

And if the poisoning was on purpose, who was doing it? Her gut instinct said it was Scottie. He had a motive—helping his girlfriend win by knocking out the competition. He also had the opportunity—delivering food to Hampton House and hanging out at the barn. Most incriminating was that blue bandana found in Show Stopper's stall the day before the thoroughbred got sick. And he could have tampered with the trail mix at the grocery store.

Yes, Jeri admitted, she really hoped it was Scottie. Otherwise it might be Mr. Petrie, and she didn't want that. He'd always been nice to her and Abby.

And yet . . .

What about the gardener's own reasons? He sounded mad at Nikki for letting her horse run through his gardens. He was also irritated with the Head for buying so much food at the grocery store. He'd said the stuff he grew was better. Was that enough reason to poison the food from Howard's? He'd had the opportunity when he was at the dorm delivering daffodils before Abby's party. He also had weed killer poisons in the greenhouse. Plus he had the knowledge about common plants that could poison people.

No matter how she arranged the puzzle pieces, something ugly was going on. It seemed most likely that someone—either living in their dorm or nearby—was systematically poisoning the girls who lived there.

She couldn't help wondering if she and Rosa would be next.

When Jeri returned to her room after school, it looked like Rosa'd opened a store. "Where'd all this stuff come from?" Jeri asked. "Not the grocery store!"

"Nope." Rosa sat cross-legged on her bed, sorting through a mound of food: packages of crackers and peanut butter, bags of miniature candy bars, chips, and small jars of salsa. "I went to the Gas-U-Up mini-mart on my bike after school." She picked up an empty chocolate cupcake wrapper, threw it toward the wastebasket, and missed. "I'm keeping this stuff in my closet."

"You're not supposed to."

"You're the one who warned me not to eat the food in the kitchen!"

"I know, but this looks like a lot of junk food for someone trying to lose a few pounds. What about carrots or apples?"

"What do you want me to do? Starve?" Rosa ripped open a package of peanut butter crackers, bit into one, and sprayed crumbs all over her bed.

"Sheesh! Don't make such a mess." Jeri picked up the wrappers and tossed them in the wastebasket. "I don't want ants and roaches crawling all over."

"Yes, boss." Rosa saluted. "Whatever you say, sir!"

Jeri sighed. "Sorry."

Rosa popped another cracker sandwich into her mouth. "You don't seem to like anything about me lately—not my clothes or my food or anything."

Jeri took a deep breath and blew it out slowly. "I guess I'm just nervous. My project is due, but it's too boring to win the scholarship. And with our friends getting poisoned, it's pretty hard to concentrate!" She grabbed her denim shorts and changed out of her school uniform, then scooped up her project papers. "I'm going downstairs to work. See ya later."

Brooke was already in the study room, her books and laptop spread over one of the tables. Jeri took the table by the window.

"What're you working on?" Brooke asked, stretching her arms behind her back.

"My article for the media fair. I need to write up my interview with Mr. Petrie yesterday."

"I'm surprised he talked to you."

"Why? Do you know him?"

"No, I only saw him Saturday when he delivered the flowers for Abby's dinner." She shrugged. "I thanked him, but he just stomped off without answering. Mean old man."

"He's usually not like that. I wonder what was bugging him."

"I don't know." Brooke mimicked his voice. "When he left, he was muttering, 'What goes around, comes around,' or something like that."

Jeri raised one eyebrow, but said nothing. Her grandpa up in Iowa used that expression lots of times. It meant you'd reap what you sowed, that there'd be consequences to pay for your actions. It *could* be taken as a threat, almost like Mr. Petrie intended revenge on somebody. Who? Nikki?

Jeri hated to believe that Mr. Petrie could be like that, but if they weren't dealing with a virus, then it had to be *somebody*, didn't it? Accidental food poisoning might happen once—and it might even affect lots of people—but it wouldn't keep happening.

After working hard on her outline before supper, Jeri wrote her rough draft after she ate. By the time she'd revised it into shape hours later, Rosa was asleep and snoring softly. She'd left Jeri's desk light on.

Rosa's snacks were on her desk, and Jeri was ravenous. One chocolate cupcake with frosting was left in an opened cellophane package. She knew Rosa would let her have it if she were awake. Jeri took it and bit into it. *Ahhh ... heaven.*

However, on the second bite, a scary thought occurred to her. It would have been so easy for someone to sneak into their unlocked dorm room while Rosa slept and tamper with the open package of snack cakes. Regretfully, Jeri tossed the rest of it into the garbage.

Still hungry, she dropped into her purple beanbag chair. She'd done her best on the article, but she knew it wasn't spectacular. Not enough to impress the judges at the media fair anyway. As she reclined on the beanbag, her mind drifted and she dozed in the quiet room.

Then her arm tickled. The skin prickled, and she jerked. "Ick!" she whispered, brushing at her arm.

She peered closely in the dim light of her desk lamp, but couldn't see anything. Then she felt the same crawly sensation up the back of her bare leg.

Covering her mouth, she suppressed a scream.

7
caught in the act

Jeri scrambled up from the beanbag and dashed for
the brightly lit hallway. She crouched down and spotted two brown ants marching up her leg. "Yuck!" She
brushed them off and stomped hard on them. Jeri sighed
in exasperation. Rosa's cupcake wrappers and cracker
crumbs were an open invitation to ants and other bugs.

Back in the room, she removed and shook out her
T-shirt and shorts, then put on pj's. First thing in the
morning, she'd make Rosa get rid of the food or store it in
a tight plastic container. Crawling under the covers, Jeri
snuggled down, muttered a quick prayer for God to kill the
ants, and then dropped off to sleep.

Over Mexican food for lunch in the dining hall
Thursday, Jeri and Rosa argued about keeping food in

their room. Finally Abby interrupted. "I'll have a good surprise for you after school if you stop fighting."

"We aren't fighting." Rosa stood abruptly. "See you later. I'll only be around a few minutes after school though."

Jeri looked up from her taco in surprise. "Why?"

"I'm going shopping with Shauna," she said casually.

"Really?" Abby asked. "Ms. Carter said you can go shopping on a school night?"

"I ran out of some stuff I need for my art fair project." Rosa shrugged and then grinned. "Can I help it if the art supply store is next to the pizza place?"

Jeri knew Shauna was old enough to drive. "Why does a girl that old want to go shopping with a sixth grader?"

"Because I'm *fun*," Rosa said, bristling. "*Some* people think I have a great sense of humor."

"I think you're funny," Jeri said, stung by her tone. She forced herself to smile. "I hope you have fun tonight," she said. "*Really.*"

Rosa paused and then flashed a huge smile. "Thanks. I will. Anything you want me to bring you?"

Jeri gave her a playful punch on the arm. "How about some bug spray?"

That evening after supper Jeri worked at her computer. She was trying—without success—to make her article exciting when Abby stuck her head in the door.

"Hey, mate, fancy a brownie?" she asked. "They'll be done in two minutes."

"You don't have to ask me twice!" Jeri shoved back from her computer and followed the blonde British girl downstairs. "Another home ec project?"

"No, Ms. Carter just said I could make some."

"So you're feeling okay now?"

"Just tired. I hate being sick." She smiled. "Brownies just sounded really good today."

Jeri grinned. "Chocolate *always* sounds good. *A chocolate brownie doeth good like a medicine*," she said, misquoting one of her mom's favorite Bible verses.

She followed Abby into the kitchen where Abby handed her a warm brownie on a paper napkin. She took a small bite. "This tastes so good," she said. "I hope you made enough."

Abby finished cutting the brownies, placed them on a plate, and grabbed a handful of paper napkins. She led the way to the living room. There five girls sat on the floor around the large coffee table, creating scrapbook pages. Jeri leaned over Emily's shoulder to see. The photos were mostly silly shots taken in the dorm of girls making goofy faces. A bowl containing a few popcorn hulls was on the floor near them.

Abby stood in the doorway. "Anybody hungry?" she asked, holding out the plate of warm brownies.

"Yum!" Brooke said, reaching for one.

Abby handed her a napkin. "I made them from scratch."

Brooke's smile faded and her hand dropped. "Actually, I'm not that hungry. I'm full of popcorn. Thanks, though."

"You can take one for later," Abby said.

"Okay."

"Here, everybody. Help yourselves." Abby handed the plate to Emily, who said, "Thanks" and passed it on without taking one. Hannah took a brownie, but she set it on the table without taking a bite.

"I guess we're all full of popcorn." Fidgeting, Emily avoided looking at Abby.

Jeri's eyes narrowed. What was going on? Abby looked confused, and then her face flushed bright pink. When it dawned on Jeri what was happening, she wanted to smack those girls. They didn't trust Abby! What did they think? That she was trying to poison them?

She grabbed the plate of brownies and stuffed another one in her mouth. "You all don't know what you're missing." She turned to Abby. "Mind if I take another one with me?"

"No. Help yourself." Abby's voice was subdued as she turned and headed upstairs.

Jeri glared at the group, but each girl stared at the scrapbooking materials on the table. Jeri wished Rosa was home. She'd eat a brownie—or several. Fuming, Jeri ran up the stairs behind Abby. She started to follow her, but Abby shook her head and disappeared into her room. She shut the door firmly. Jeri stood in the hallway, finished the third brownie, and then headed to her own room.

This was going too far. It was bad enough that Abby felt guilty about serving some spoiled food last weekend.

Now the girls acted like she was doing something to their food on purpose! What were they thinking? *I have to get to the bottom of this now.* At this rate, Abby wouldn't want to come back next year. And to Jeri, Abby was the best thing about the Landmark School for Girls.

By the time Rosa got back at 9:30, Jeri was ready for bed. Rosa dropped a neon pink shopping bag on her bed. Jeri started telling her about the girls' reactions to Abby's brownies—but her voice drifted off when she realized Rosa wasn't listening.

Jeri studied her friend's serious expression. "Anything the matter?"

"No." Rosa sniffed. "What stinks in here?"

"Ant spray. I got some from Ms. Carter." Jeri peered closer. "What's wrong? Did something happen?"

Rosa shook her head and went to stand before the mirror. Jeri studied her friend's reflection. Her tan legs and bare arms showed no signs of injury that Jeri could see.

"Did you and Shauna have a fight?" Jeri finally asked.

"No." Rosa gulped. "Shauna wasn't even there when it happened."

"When *what* happened?"

Rosa wrapped her arms around herself. "It was at the pizzeria. Shauna went to the restroom to wash sauce off her shorts, and I was by myself eating breadsticks." She paused and a shudder passed through her. "Then these two guys—high school, I guess—came over to our booth. One sat real close beside me and the other one across from me."

Jeri held her breath for a moment, bracing herself. "Then what?"

"They called me *babe* and said there was a party they wanted to take me to. I told them no, and they just laughed. The one beside me scooted so close I could smell his stinky breath." She glanced at Jeri in alarm. "I was smashed against the wall and couldn't get away from him."

Jeri's stomach knotted in fear as she imagined the scene. If she'd been trapped by two high school creeps, she'd have been too paralyzed to even scream. "What'd you do?"

"I told them to leave me alone!" Her eyes flashed with anger then. "You know what they said? They told me to stop playing innocent. Then that creep put his hand on my leg!"

Jeri's heart hammered. "Did he hurt you?"

"No. Shauna came back then and told them to get lost or she'd call mall security. They said they'd be looking for me later, but they left." She sighed. "I don't know why they bothered *me*."

Jeri hugged Rosa and said, "I'm so sorry that happened. I'm so glad Shauna came back to help you get rid of those creeps. Are you okay?" She could feel Rosa relax as Jeri held her a moment longer.

Rosa nodded. "I'm gonna take a quick shower."

Jeri crawled in bed and snuggled down into her pillow when Rosa left the room. Lying there, she imagined what Rosa had gone through with those boys and thanked God that she was only frightened. If Shauna hadn't shown up when she did, it could have turned out much worse. Rosa might be interested in attracting boys, but she didn't deserve that kind of attention! Jeri already knew what kind of guy she wanted someday. The *Dallas* kind.

Whenever Jeri brought up the subject of boys at home, her mom usually reminded her of a verse in 1 Peter. Your beauty "should be that of your inner self, the unfading beauty of a gentle and quiet spirit, which is of great worth in God's sight." Would a gentle and quiet spirit really be enough though? It was kinda hard for Jeri to believe. Sure, God thought those traits were worth a lot, but would some boy?

As she lay there, her mind drifted to the people she liked best at Landmark School, like Abby and Rosa and Ms. Carter and Emily. What traits did she admire about them? Well ... they were friendly, always ready to help, encouraging when she was down. None of those traits, Jeri realized, had anything to do with looks. Not a single one. Abby and Rosa were definitely cute, but that wasn't what Jeri valued about them.

Jeri rolled over, throwing her arm over her eyes. What was taking Rosa so long in the bathroom? Probably telling her story to every girl who came in there.

Each time Jeri closed her eyes, she pictured the high school boys harassing Rosa, or Nikki being taken to the infirmary, or the girls refusing to eat Abby's brownies, or Claire claiming Sierra would win the scholarship.

Jeri tossed back and forth. By the time Rosa came back, Jeri was wide awake. Just minutes later, Rosa was sound asleep, hugging a stuffed bunny. Jeri stared at the patterns of shifting light on the ceiling made from trees outside swaying in the breeze.

The giant red numbers on her digital clock changed, slowly but surely. Mentally she reviewed the order of events. Saturday night—just five nights ago—Abby fixed the birthday supper and five girls (including herself) got sick. Nikki spent the night in the infirmary. Monday night she found Brooke sick again in the restroom. After breakfast on Tuesday, some girls and Miss Barbara were sick, and Abby went to the infirmary. Tuesday evening Emily, Brooke, and Nikki watched the movie together, ate trail mix, and got sick—with Emily landing in the hospital. Jeri had learned from Mr. Petrie that some common plants were poisonous, so the poisonings could have been accidental. But could so *many* incidents be accidental?

But if it was on purpose, why?

With so many getting sick, it was impossible to tell who was targeted. Was one girl the intended victim, and the rest of the girls poisoned to confuse everyone? It did make it look more like a virus that way.

Jeri went over the possibilities in her mind. Nikki could be the target. She got the sickest after the birthday dinner, putting her in danger of not being able to compete on Saturday. Then she got sick again on the trail mix. There were probably several girls besides Janeen who needed to win that horse show scholarship.

Or had Nikki simply made someone mad enough to take revenge? Nikki could be more abrasive than sandpaper on an open sore. An angry girl might not fight back directly, since Nikki was bigger than most everybody. But poisoning the food would certainly be great revenge.

Jeri flopped over on her stomach. It might not be an angry *girl* either. It sounded like Mr. Petrie and Nikki had an argument when Show Stopper got loose, and Nikki even complained to the Head about him. What had Brooke overheard him say when he delivered the flowers? *What goes around, comes around?* That might have meant nothing, but it could have been a threat.

Jeri curled up in a ball, disturbed by the direction of her thoughts. She *liked* Mr. Petrie. But other ideas crowded in. Like he grew some of the vegetables they ate. Could Mr. Petrie have slipped some poison foods into the basket that Scottie delivered when he brought the daffodils for Abby's party? Jeri hated to believe such a thing. *Dear God, what is the truth here?* Jeri tossed and turned, stirring up more questions than finding answers.

Finally she gave up trying to sleep. For one thing, her stomach was growling. She needed something to eat.

She tried Rosa's snack box first. Empty wrappers were mixed with dead ants. Shuddering, she dumped it in the wastebasket. It was way past eleven—the official stay-in-your-room hour—but she was starving. She'd be quick.

Jeri tiptoed down the carpeted stairs in the dimly lit hall, feeling like a burglar. In the kitchen, she flipped on the overhead light and squinted till her eyes adjusted to the brightness.

What did she want? Cereal or graham crackers, she decided, if she could find a safe, unopened package.

In the pantry she found several boxes and opened a new package of cinnamon graham crackers. She wasn't taking any chances on the open boxes. She grabbed out five or six large crackers and bit off a piece, returning the box to the shelf and closing the pantry door.

Back in the kitchen, she turned slowly, studying the cupboard doors as she munched. Each girl had a small shelf of her own for personal snacks, with her name on a card taped to her cupboard door. Jeri's shelf was near the back door. She shared a cupboard with Rosa, Abby, and Nikki. Each girl also had a clearly labeled white plastic container for perishable snacks in the giant refrigerator. Jeri's was empty now. She'd thrown away everything after Nikki got sick.

She wondered what everyone else had in their cupboard and refrigerator space. There'd never be a better time to investigate. If she looked, could she tell if something was suspicious? Maybe. She'd sure check out anyone with green potatoes, rhubarb leaves, and mushrooms!

But when she looked, the plastic containers in the double-wide refrigerator contained nothing more suspicious than some yogurt, cheese sticks, and candy bars. Not really surprising, she decided. Would a poisoner be stupid enough to leave her poison in plain sight?

Quietly and quickly, she opened cupboard doors and poked among the girls' things: cookies, Pop Tarts, birthday candles, cans of soup, chips, and kettle corn. She had just opened Brooke and Emily's cupboard when she heard a shuffling noise behind her. She whipped around, her heart pounding.

"What are you doing?" Emily's voice barely carried across the room.

Jeri's heart sank at the sight of her frightened expression. How in the world was she going to explain this?

8

setting a trap

Jeri gulped.

Emily stared wide-eyed at her own cupboard door, now standing open. "What are you doing?" she asked again.

"I came down for some crackers." Jeri tried to keep her voice light and nudged the door shut with her elbow. "You hungry too?"

"No." She paused. "When I went to the bathroom, I saw you going downstairs and wondered if you were okay."

"Just hungry." Jeri moved away from Emily's cupboard, but Emily remained standing in the doorway. Jeri wished the cracker box was on the counter to make her story look true. She could tell what Emily was thinking. *What are you doing in my cupboard when your own is way over by the back door?*

Emily glanced over her shoulder. "You'll get in trouble for being down here so late."

"I don't think Ms. Carter would want me to starve."

"Probably not." Emily seemed to consider that. "I've been working on my science fair project. It's chilly in our room."

"Want some hot chocolate? You have a couple packets left." Jeri could have kicked herself the moment the words left her mouth. Why not just announce that she'd searched Emily's cupboard?

"Um, no." Emily looked at Jeri, and then glanced quickly away. Her fingers twisted the hem of her shorty pajamas into knots. "Good night, Jeri."

"I'll come too." Jeri reached to turn out the overhead light. Before she touched the switch, Emily had turned and fled from the kitchen. In a moment Jeri heard her taking the stairs two at a time.

Oh, brother, Jeri thought, following more slowly. *Did she think I was going to hurt her? Now what should I do?*

On Friday morning Jeri yawned as the Hampton House girls lined up two by two to walk to the dining hall for breakfast. Jeri noticed Emily and Brooke watching her. Jeri tried to catch Emily's eye to smile at her, but each time Emily turned another direction.

I wasn't doing anything! Jeri wanted to scream. But if she tried to explain why she'd been snooping through everyone's food, it would only make her sound guilty. And yet, Jeri hated the idea that Emily might suspect *her* now. Brooke did too. She could tell by the way she was stealing dark glances at her. No doubt Emily had told her room-mate where she'd found Jeri in the middle of the night.

In her library period that morning, Jeri couldn't concentrate. She had the nagging feeling that she was missing something important. *God, what is it?* Had she seen something in the cupboards or the refrigerator that hadn't sunk in? Maybe some of those foods *could* be poisonous under certain conditions. In the computer room next door, she researched more on food poisoning. Although she learned a lot about correct food storage and symptoms of poisoning, none of it was helpful.

She slumped in her chair, wishing she could talk to her mom. But Mrs. McKane was on a business trip in Indiana, giving speeches at a sales conference. Jeri didn't want to interrupt her presentation. She sighed. Email was better than nothing.

She signed into her email and typed as fast as she could. She didn't want her mom to freak out about a poisoner on the loose in her dorm. So instead, she wrote about Rosa and the high school boys at the pizza place. "I don't want that kind of attention. Even so, I wish I got noticed too. You'll think I'm terrible—"

Just then an instant message popped up on her screen.

ImHis: What luck! I was just checking email and saw your smiley face icon lit up. Glad you're online.

Jerichogirl: HI I ROT U EM

ImHis: Whoa! Plain English, okay? No text message gobbledy-gook!

Jerichogirl: sorry—I wrote you an email—let me send it now.

Jeri pushed Send and waited for her mom to read it.

ImHis: No, I don't think you're terrible. You're normal! That's a good thing. I just think you're maybe asking the wrong question.

Jerichogirl: what do U mean??????????

ImHis: Do you want the attention of a boy who only goes for mini skirts and tight shirts?

Jerichogirl: no—but I don't like 2 B invisible either.

ImHis: Think about this—what kind of boy do you want attention from?

Jerichogirl: easy—the kind that treats U like a lady—a guy that's fun 2 do stuff with—a guy who isn't fake.

ImHis: Fake?

Jerichogirl: one who only acts like a Christian at church.

ImHis: Great list there! Boys like that make excellent friends. So ... next thing to do is ask yourself this: Am I the kind of girl this kind of guy would like for a friend?

Jerichogirl: U don't understand—I don't need more guy friends—I wish I could be more than a friend.

ImHis: Well, in sixth grade, you're too young to have boys be anything more than friends. I know it's not a popular thing to say, but it's true. Learn to be friends with boys. Boys who are good friends now make good boyfriends later, when you're old enough to date. Much later, they also make good husbands.

Jerichogirl: I guess, but that's a long time away.

ImHis: Yes, there's PLENTY of time. You want to attract quality boys when the time is right, sweetie. Your job now is to grow into the kind of quality girl the Bible talks about. Fruity, right?

Jeri smiled then. *Fruity* was her mom's expression for showing the fruits of the Spirit: love, joy, peace, patience, kindness, goodness, faithfulness, gentleness, and self-control. Startled, she realized that those words pretty well described Dallas.

Jerichogirl: I NO UR right—but fruity girls don't get much notice.

ImHis: I won't lie to you. It's true that you won't get noticed by as many boys if you dress modestly and concentrate on developing good character. But when you DO get attention, it will be for the right reasons and from the right boys. It just takes time—which you have plenty of.

Jerichogirl: in fact I don't—gotta go.

ImHis: Okay. You go ahead, but check email later.

Just then the bell rang, and Jeri logged off. Sighing, she wished she could put boys out of her mind altogether for a couple years.

After her second period class, she ran back to the computer lab and found the email from her mom.

> Sorry we got cut off this morning. In your email you
> mentioned Rosa's clothes and her beautiful black hair
> several times. We all envy others' looks sometimes,
> but work hard to be satisfied with how God made you.
> You're beautiful—in God's eyes as well as mine. Try to
> really believe this truth: a gentle, peaceful spirit is more
> becoming at any age than any clothing you could wear

or any hairstyle. "The Lord does not look at the things [human beings look] at. [People] look at the outward appearance, but the Lord looks at the heart" (1 Samuel 16:7). Don't let the world dictate how you feel about yourself.

Jeri reread the email, then closed it. At gut level, she knew her mom was right, but sometimes it was so hard. God might look at her heart, but *people* looked at the outside. If they didn't like what they saw, would they bother getting to know her heart? What was wrong with having a good heart *and* a great "outside"? Surely she could have both, couldn't she? Yes, she wanted to please God, but she wanted to look pleasing to others too. She sighed. If only it didn't matter to her.

But since knowing Dallas, it *did* matter.

A lot.

Jeri spent the rest of the school day with her busy mind going from one problem to another — and missing half of what her teachers said. She wanted to figure out what was going on in the dorm. Ms. Carter seemed content to blame a virus, but some of the girls acted like Abby was guilty of poisoning people. Jeri figured she had moved up to the number-one-suspect position herself after Emily caught her snooping in the kitchen. She had to get rid of the cloud of suspicion that floated over them.

Throughout the day, Jeri brainstormed ways to spice up her accidental food poisoning report, but nothing worthwhile came to her. Time was critical, or that slick chick Sierra Sedgewick would win the media fair competition with her dad's photos. Talk about unfair!

It wasn't until Friday's last class that an idea occurred to Jeri that just might trap the culprit. Suddenly alert and focused, she considered her plan from all angles.

Yes. It ought to work. But to be effective, she couldn't tell anyone her plan.

On Friday nights, Hampton House ordered food from the pizzeria to be delivered at six. The girls ate pizza and then played cards or board games. Winners of the friendly competitions received coupons from the house mothers for things like "one hour of video games" or "one-hour extension of lights out." It'd be a perfect night to try her plan.

That evening Jeri waited at the front door until the pizza was delivered and paid for by Ms. Carter. She guarded it till supper, then was careful to eat from all three pizza boxes: pepperoni, Hawaiian, and beef. Half an hour into the *UNO* competition, she pressed on her stomach and tried to look ill.

No one noticed.

A few minutes later, she grabbed her stomach and groaned. Jumping up, she dashed to the first-floor bathroom. She slammed the door, made some barfing noises, and flushed the toilet twice. Ms. Carter was outside the bathroom when she opened the door, with Abby and Rosa behind her.

"Oh dear," Ms. Carter said, putting her arm around Jeri's waist. "Looks like you've caught the bug too." She felt Jeri's forehead, and Jeri tried to look weak. "No fever. That's a good sign. We'd better get you to bed."

"But I'm okay now."

"Are you sure?" Ms. Carter said. "Miss Barbara could sit with you upstairs."

"No. Really. I'd rather finish the game. I was winning." Going upstairs would wreck her plan. Jeri padded back into the living room, where the girls looked at her. Trying not to be obvious, Jeri glanced at each girl. Did anyone look shocked that she was sick? The poisoner would know the pizza hadn't been tampered with, so she'd guess that Jeri was pretending. Would she give herself away?

"Does anyone else feel sick?" Jeri asked. "I think there's something wrong with the pizza."

The girls looked at each other and Ms. Carter, shaking their heads. The house mother told them to let her know if any of them felt nauseated.

Brooke fanned out her handful of cards. "Is this your first time getting sick?"

Jeri nodded. "I guess I'm pretty healthy."

Brooke tapped her cards in her palm. "You should get more sleep. You pick up germs and viruses quicker when you're tired."

Should get more sleep? What was she hinting at? Jeri glanced at Emily, who looked alarmed and then stared at the floor. Emily had obviously reported that Jeri was in the kitchen during the night.

"Actually I don't believe it's a virus." Jeri took a deep breath. "I think someone in this dorm is poisoning our food." Two girls who were tallying the score sheets jerked around. "On purpose."

Brooke pointed at Jeri. "And maybe it's *you*, faking sick tonight so no one will think *you're* behind it all." She glanced at Emily, then back at Jeri. "We know what you do when everyone else is asleep."

Nervous questions flew back and forth, and the card tournament was forgotten. Ms. Carter and Miss Barbara shushed everyone, but it didn't help. Finally the house mother stood. "Go back to the game, girls," Ms. Carter said. "Jeri, you and Brooke come with me. Emily, you too."

"I'm coming too," Rosa whispered.

"Thanks." Jeri shuddered, now feeling sick for real. This wasn't how she'd planned it! She thought her little trick would shock the real poisoner into giving herself away. Instead, she looked guiltier than ever!

"Let's go to Jeri and Rosa's room," Ms. Carter said, leading the way.

When in the room, she motioned for them all to sit on the floor. She sat on Rosa's desk chair. "Everyone, take a few deep breaths." She waited a moment. "We evidently have a misunderstanding. It's been a stressful week for everyone, with so many being ill and the pressures of final projects." She rubbed the back of her neck. "Let's start with you, Brooke. What did you mean about unusual activities during the night?"

"Well, I didn't actually see her, but Emily did." Brooke poked Emily in the arm. "You tell them."

Emily stared at the floor. "I didn't really see Jeri doing anything."

"Yes, you did!" Brooke said.

Emily looked at Jeri, both fear and regret on her face. "I went down to the kitchen in the middle of the night last night," she whispered. "I was on the way to the bathroom when I saw Jeri going downstairs. I followed her."

"And ...?" Ms. Carter asked.

Emily picked at a loose thread on her sweatshirt cuff. "And I found Jeri in the kitchen."

Brooke rolled her eyes. "Tell Ms. Carter exactly *where* you found Jeri while everyone in the dorm was sleeping."

Emily looked miserable, and Jeri felt sorry for her. She was caught between telling the truth and not wanting to get a friend in trouble.

Jeri cleared her throat. "That's okay. I'll tell her." She sighed. "I was in Emily and Brooke's cupboard."

9
backfired

Ms. Carter frowned and covered her mouth for a moment. Finally she asked Jeri, "What were you doing in someone else's cupboard?"

"And in the middle of the night!" Brooke said.

"Brooke, please. You've had your turn. Let Jeri answer."

Jeri cleared her throat. "I checked out everyone's cupboard, not just theirs, looking for things someone might use to put in our food. Abby felt rotten about her birthday supper making some girls sick, but I knew it wasn't her fault. I wanted to discover who was behind it—or if *anyone* was."

"That's not the real reason." Brooke shook her head in disgust. "You're writing about food poisoning for the media fair. So you frame someone by planting a poison in their cupboard, then you 'discover' it and write about it. All this just to win a prize!"

"You take that back!" Rosa said. "Jeri's the most honest person I know."

Jeri's heart pounded. "I didn't put anything in anyone's cupboard. Honest."

"That's enough, girls. Flinging accusations around isn't helpful. The thing is ..." Ms. Carter paused. "The thing is, Jeri, if you *had* found something suspicious, you *could* be accused of planting the evidence yourself in order to make someone else look guilty."

"I never thought of that," Jeri mumbled. She should have taken Rosa and Abby with her as witnesses.

The house mother reached down and patted Jeri's shoulder. "If it helps you to know, I've checked the cupboards and fridge myself every day. I've also kept in touch with the local police and a doctor. We *are* taking these incidents seriously." Ms. Carter paused. "The doctor feels it's a virus, and we need to wash our hands better so we don't spread it around. I tend to agree."

Jeri didn't respond, but she felt strongly that it was more than that. "I'm sorry I faked being sick tonight," she said. "I was hoping to shock the guilty person into saying something, but I guess it backfired."

"I know," the house mother said, "but it's over now."

A few minutes later, after the others left, Jeri flopped back on her bed and rubbed her abdomen. "My stomach really *does* hurt now," she said. "Did you see how Brooke and Emily looked at me when they left? They think *I'm* poisoning people!"

Rosa shook her head. "Then they don't have the brains of a toad."

Jeri laughed. "Thanks for sticking up for me."

Rosa dug in her closet, found her heating pad, and plugged it in. After turning it on, she placed it on Jeri's stomach. "I know we don't agree on everything, but you wouldn't hurt anyone. That much I know after living with you all year."

"I'm sorry for bugging you about your clothes lately," Jeri said.

"It's okay." Rosa sat cross-legged on her own bed and faced her. "I've been thinking about the clothes I've been wearing lately. You know those boys at the pizza place? I didn't make them act like jerks, but I can see why they *might* think I wanted attention." She sighed. "I think I'm going to return some of the outfits I bought online."

"Really?" Jeri pressed the heating pad against her stomach, relaxing in its warmth.

"Yeah. I think ... maybe ... I've worried too much about clothes lately. I read a magazine today in the library, and it had this huge survey somebody did."

"What kind?"

"About friendship. They gave the survey to a thousand girls, asking them what they valued in a friend." She wrapped her arms around her bent knees. " 'Somebody who wears cool clothes' wasn't even on the list."

Jeri grinned. She wasn't surprised. "Do you remember what ranked the highest?"

"Um, loyalty and kindness and a good smile. Being fun with a good sense of humor ranked real high too."

"That's you exactly! Hampton House would vote you as the girl with the best smile who's the most fun," Jeri said. "Where did a girl's looks rank on the list?"

"Appearance was close to the bottom, but it was about being clean and neat, not about wearing hot clothes."

Jeri cupped her hands under her head and stared at the ceiling. "That survey's right," she said. "I needed a friend when Brooke was accusing me. And I cared a lot more that you were loyal than what kind of jeans you had on."

Rosa grinned. "Okay, so remember that the next time you get ants in your pants."

On Saturday morning, Jeri woke up before six a.m. Rosa was still asleep, and from the stillness of the dorm, so were most other girls. Between the mockingbird outside their window and her worries over the poisoning, there was no chance of going back to sleep. Jeri gave up and crawled out of bed. She went downstairs for a while, but she felt antsy and cooped up. Maybe getting out and walking would help her think.

Outside ten minutes later, she strolled toward the bell tower, her mind skipping from one problem to another. *God, I can't make sense out of anything. What am I missing?* She went around the corner of the bell tower and almost bumped into Sierra Sedgwick.

"Hey, Jeri!" Dressed in pink and white jogging shorts and a tank, Sierra had her long hair up tight in a ponytail. She stopped in front of Jeri and jogged in place.

"Hi, Sierra." Sierra looked perfect, as always. And there wasn't any sweat on Sierra's face, neck, or shirt. "So, I heard you're entering a photo book for the media fair."

"You heard right." Sierra's smile was bright, her teeth perfect. Rosa claimed she wore whitening strips to bed every night. Then Sierra's face clouded over. "At least, I hope I am. I'm still waiting for something to come in the mail for it." She caught her lower lip between her teeth. "It just *has* to get here today."

"What is it?"

"Um, some material for the book cover."

Jeri cocked her head to one side. That sounded odd. Why would material come in the mail? Jeri wondered. Was it possible that Rosa was right, and Sierra's dad was sending his photos for *her* project? Maybe they were late. Hope surged in Jeri. If the package of pictures didn't arrive by Monday, Sierra would be out of the competition!

"Don't jog too hard," Jeri said. "See you Monday night."

When Jeri got back to the dorm, the hallway just inside the front door was jammed with bags and boxes and posters. Abby, Emily, and Brooke were getting their displays for the science fair ready to set up at the Sports Center gym today. That evening from seven to ten, each student would give a ten-minute presentation for the judges.

Upstairs, Rosa was still in bed, reading a magazine and eating a package of cheesy crackers. "Boy, you were up early."

"Went for a walk." Jeri dropped onto her desk chair and straddled it backwards to look at Rosa. "I have to finish my article today. Want to walk over to the greenhouse with me? I want to borrow another book."

"Sure." Rosa hopped off her bed, tossed aside her magazine, and slipped on her flip-flops. Jeri didn't comment on it, but she noticed that today Rosa was dressed in a looser T-shirt and denim capris. She still looked totally cool.

It was warming up already, and Jeri and Rosa strolled along, talking about summer plans. It was a relief to Jeri to think about something besides poison for a while. Circling around the statue in front of Herald Hall, they bumped into Sierra.

"Wow! Two times in one morning," Sierra drawled. "Are you following me?" Her smile was blinding now.

What's with her? Jeri wondered. Earlier she'd seemed anxious.

"What's that?" Rosa asked, poking a large envelope sticking out of Sierra's backpack. It was an express mailer—the kind *rush-rush* mail came in.

"Something I needed for my media fair project," Sierra said, dimpling. "It just came."

Jeri's hope deflated like a leaky balloon. That size mailer could definitely hold a dozen 8" x 10" photos.

"Well, good luck on Monday," Jeri forced herself to say.

"May the best girl win," Rosa added brightly. When they were out of earshot, she whispered to Jeri, "And that's *you*. I bet that package was photos from her dad. There's no point in working so hard when there're girls like Sierra in the world."

Jeri didn't reply. She could only hope Rosa was wrong.

At the next fork in the sidewalk, they turned left toward the Sports Center. People were still carrying in posters and displays for the science fair. Coming toward them, head down, was Brooke. She was dressed in jeans so tight Jeri could see a rock or something in her front pocket. Deep in thought, Brooke barely noticed them.

They continued down the rock path to the greenhouse and stepped inside the dim front building. Jeri called to Mr. Petrie, but there was no answer. "His bookshelf is in an office at the back. I think it'd be okay to get another book and leave him a note."

In the office Jeri studied the titles on the shelves. Rosa strolled around the little room, reading the notes tacked to the various bulletin boards. Framed certificates, awards, and newspaper articles lined one whole wall. Jeri had just found two books when Rosa whistled shrilly.

"Look what I found." She was standing by Mr. Petrie's open desk drawer, waving a paper.

"What is it?"

"A warning. Look!"

"You shouldn't be in his desk!" Jeri glanced over her

shoulder to make sure Mr. Petrie wasn't coming. Then curiosity got the best of her. "Warning for what?"

"It's a report from the Head," Rosa said. "It says here that 'Yelling at a student is conduct unbecoming to a staff member of Landmark School for Girls.'"

"I wonder who he yelled at."

"Um, let me see." Rosa's finger slid down the paper. "It was Nikki! Come here. She said he yelled and swore at her when her horse got into his garden." She whistled softly. "And down here at the bottom ... look!"

Jeri hurried across the little office. "What?"

"See who signed the complaint?" She pointed at the signature.

"Ms. Carter?" Confused, Jeri leaned close to read. It said the house mother had reported the incident on behalf of one of her girls, Nikki Brown. It was a formal complaint lodged against Mr. Petrie, and it said Mr. Petrie was on probation for it. Jeri glanced over her shoulder again. "Put that back before he comes in and catches us."

"Okay, okay."

"Let's get outta here." As they hurried to the glassed-in area full of plants, Jeri filled her in on what she knew. They stopped in the shade of some hanging ferns.

Rosa's voice dropped to a whisper. "Maybe he wants revenge on both Nikki *and* Ms. Carter."

Jeri nodded. "Plus, adding something poisonous to Scottie's groceries makes the grocery store look bad."

"Why would he care about that?"

Jeri's heart felt heavy, like something was sitting on her chest. "A few days ago Mr. Petrie said the Head should be serving more of the food he grew because his was better than the store's."

"Is that a big deal?"

"I don't know." Jeri shrugged. "Maybe he gets paid extra for growing the food for the dining hall. Using Howard's would cut into his income then."

Rosa touched a delicate-looking ivory orchid. "What should we do?"

"Nothing right now." Jeri peered through the smudged glass walls of the greenhouse looking for Mr. Petrie. "I think I see him watering out there. I need to tell him about borrowing his book. Be right back."

Outside she walked alongside some miniature garden plots. Then she cut across and made her way between rows of huge white waxy flowers, reminding herself to act natural. "Hi, Mr. Petrie," she called.

He glanced toward her and waved. "What's up?"

"Can I borrow this book next for my report?" Jeri's lips felt stiff, and she hoped her smile looked halfway normal.

"Sure. Just bring it back soon." When Jeri didn't move, he said, "Anything else?"

Tongue-tied and mouth dry, Jeri was vaguely aware of bees buzzing in the blooms. Yes, there was something else, but she could hardly ask, *Have you poisoned any girls this week?*

"No. Nothing. Thanks."

She pivoted, sliding in the newly watered dirt, and went down. *Hard.* She felt a crunch in her ankle when she landed. Large blossoms lay under her in the mud, and a mad bumblebee zipped around her head. Jeri swatted at it and missed. The sting on her neck made her howl with pain.

"Ow!" she cried. Her neck suddenly felt as if it were on fire.

Mr. Petrie helped her to her feet and then picked up his book. "You all right?" he asked, handing her the paperback.

"My neck!" Jeri said, touching it tenderly. A bump was already swelling.

"Come with me. I've got a first-aid kit in my office."

The painful burning was worsening, but Jeri wasn't going inside with Mr. Petrie. Not after the warning she'd read. "I'll just go back to my dorm," Jeri said. "It's not so bad now. Really."

But Jeri needed to get Rosa first. She turned down a mowed path between the tiny garden plots. A few empty ones were tilled and raked smooth. The others held plants more than half grown. Labeled stakes marked rows of radishes, zinnias, and peas. Name plates were stuck in the ground at each plot.

Glancing at them as she hurried by, Jeri spotted one that said *Brooke.* She wondered who it was. There were lots of Brookes at Landmark. When Jeri poked her head inside the greenhouse, Rosa was reclining on a bag of cedar chips.

"There you are," Rosa said. "Wanna come with me to

the library?" Rosa stood and brushed off the seat of her pants. "I'm checking out some horsey DVD for Nikki." She pointed at Jeri's muddy legs. "What happened to you?"

"I fell, and then I got stung." She pointed to her neck. "I'm going back to the dorm to get something for it. I'll meet you back there, okay?"

Ten minutes later when Jeri entered Hampton House, the grandfather clock in the living room was chiming. She hoped Ms. Carter was in her office. Then she heard the house mother's deep laugh coming from the kitchen, and she headed down the hall.

She was almost to the kitchen when she also heard Emily's voice, then Brooke's. Jeri pulled back from the kitchen doorway. She wanted to ask Ms. Carter to check her bee sting—it was really throbbing—but not with Brooke and Emily there.

Jeri waited in the hallway, hoping they'd leave soon. She listened as the girls described some of the science fair displays.

"I'm petrified about tonight," Emily said. "If only I knew what the judges were going to ask! Then I could practice my answers."

"You'll do fine," Ms. Carter said. "Remember, everyone else will be in the same boat, having to answer off the top of their heads."

"Yup," Brooke agreed. "I'm nervous too. At least you know Ms. Todd thinks your project has a great chance of winning."

"She was just being nice," Emily protested.

"Whatever!" Brooke said. "She didn't say that to me!"

"I guess we'll find out tonight," Emily said. "For now, I just want to take a break and veg out. We're allowing ourselves twenty minutes."

"What are you girls eating?" Ms. Carter said.

"Salsa and chips," Brooke said.

"I love salsa—but not the spicy stuff," Emily added. "I got four jars at the store." She laughed. "I'm eating this whole little jar myself!"

"Mine's got hot peppers." It sounded to Jeri like Brooke smacked her lips. "We kept all the food in our room this week though, just in case."

"For now, girls, that's probably wise," Ms. Carter said. Footsteps crossed the tile floor. "I need to get something from my car. I'll be right back." The kitchen door opened and closed.

Emily said, "Grab a tray, okay? I'll start the movie. At least we can watch the beginning."

Oh no, Jeri thought. *Please no.* They weren't going to eat their snack in the kitchen. And now they'd catch her lurking on their way to the TV room. She scanned the area for a place to hide. Where? The hall closet. Or maybe—

Too late.

Emily came around the corner, carrying a jar of salsa and a can of soda, and nearly collided with Jeri before skidding to a stop. Brooke plowed into Emily's back and dropped the bag of chips.

"What are you doing?" Brooke demanded when she spotted Jeri. "Let me guess. Spying!"

10

safe at last

"I wasn't spying," Jeri mumbled. "I wanted to talk to Ms. Carter."

Of course, she *had* been eavesdropping. She stooped to pick up the spilled chips. Handing them to Brooke, Jeri saw that Brooke's palm was spotted with a rash again. *I'm glad I don't have allergies,* she thought.

The kitchen door opened and closed then, and Ms. Carter was back. Jeri went to show her the bee sting. While Ms. Carter cleaned it and applied antibiotic cream, Jeri's mind began to wander. Something was bothering her—she couldn't put her finger on it—but it buzzed around her head like that bumblebee.

"Are you all right?" Ms. Carter asked. "You seem a little dazed." She felt Jeri's forehead. "Bee stings can be serious. Are you sick to your stomach?"

"I don't think so ..."

Jeri closed her eyes and did an instant replay of the last five minutes. In slow motion she reviewed the conversation she'd overheard, then running into Brooke and Emily, picking up the chips and handing them back to Brooke ... What was wrong? What had set her mind to churning?

"I think I might lie down for a while," Jeri finally said.

She headed upstairs, thoughts whirling in confusion. Maybe a nap would help. First she walked by Brooke and Emily's room. When she walked by the partially opened door, a pungent odor wafted out. Jeri blinked. What was that strong smell?

Glancing around the room, she couldn't see anything odd enough to account for the odor. Then she noticed the wastebasket. The smell seemed to be drifting up from there. She inspected the contents and found a spoon with bits of red sauce on it. She sniffed again. *Salsa.*

But that didn't account for the whole smell.

Jeri turned slowly, sniffing, and then bent down, reaching under the edge of the nearest bed. She pulled out a wad of paper towels, unwrapped them, and saw what looked like a garlic press. Her mom used one when she cooked homemade spaghetti sauce. She picked it up and smelled it. The white bits left in the press sure didn't smell like garlic.

What could it be? And why did the plastic spoon have salsa on it? Had something been added to the salsa? It wasn't garlic, but something that could be crushed in the garlic press.

Then, unbidden, an image of Brooke's tight jeans and the lump in her pocket flashed through Jeri's mind. Downstairs just now, when she'd handed Brooke the spilled chips, there was no lump in her front pocket. She must have done something with—

"Oh no!"

Jeri dashed out of the room and down the hall and, hanging onto the banister, flew down the stairs. She bumped into Ms. Carter in the entryway, but there was no time to explain.

In the TV room, the movie had begun. Emily and Brooke were sprawled on the lumpy couch, feet up on the coffee table. A tray of food was between them. Emily had opened her jar of salsa and dipped her tortilla chip full. She had her mouth open wide.

Jeri flung herself into the room, leaped over Brooke's legs, and knocked the chip from Emily's hand. "Don't eat that!" she cried.

Emily screamed. Brooke yelled and hit Jeri's back. Jeri cracked one shin so hard on the edge of the coffee table that it took her breath away. She bounced and rolled onto the floor, landing on Emily's feet and whacking her elbow on the floor.

"What are you *doing?*" Brooke yelled, standing over her.

Jeri tried to take deep breaths, willing the pain to subside. Her arm and leg were bent awkwardly under her.

She heard steps running down the hall, and several girls pounding down the stairs called, "What's going on?"

Jeri rolled over, rubbing her elbow and arm. Then she grabbed the jars of salsa before Brooke could. "Here," she said breathlessly, handing them to Ms. Carter. "If you have these tested, I think you'll see that Brooke's jar of salsa is fine—but Emily's has been poisoned."

Emily gasped.

"You're crazy," Brooke said. "You're trying to frame *me* now!"

Ms. Carter helped Jeri up to a chair, then—setting the salsa on the table—said, "I think you'd better explain." She felt Jeri's forehead again.

"No, I'm *not* running a fever. I know what I'm saying." She rubbed her shin. "When you test that salsa, I think you'll find more than onions or garlic in it. I think you'll find a crushed daffodil bulb."

The color drained slowly from Brooke's face. "You're crazy!" she said, turning to the doorway.

"Stay put, please." Ms. Carter's voice had a steely edge. "Let's get to the bottom of this. Jeri, what in the world are you talking about?"

"Check Brooke's palms, Ms. Carter."

Brooke frowned at her hands. "It's a rash. You already know I have allergies."

"I know you *told* me Monday night that you had allergies. That's when you heard me go into the bathroom and rushed in after me, pretending to be sick."

"I wasn't pretending to be sick!"

"Well, you made a lot of gagging noises anyway, to throw suspicion off yourself. You sure didn't want me to get Ms. Carter that night."

"I told you why!" Brooke spluttered.

"You told me lots of things," Jeri said. "Today at the greenhouse I saw a garden plot with your name by it. It reminded me that you use daffodils in your science display."

"So?"

"So if we look in your room, would you have any daffodil bulbs up there?"

"No."

Emily's voice was soft—and confused. "But you got some today."

Brooke turned on her in fury. "So what! I used them for my science fair project. You know that."

Ms. Carter stepped forward then. "Jeri, I'm not following you. What does Brooke's science fair project have to do with this salsa?"

"Nothing," Jeri said, "except I saw Brooke earlier. I thought she was on the way home from setting up at the gym, but she was actually coming back from the greenhouse. She had a lump in her pants pocket then, like a rock." She pointed at Brooke's front pocket. "It's not there now. I'm betting that the 'rock' was a daffodil bulb from the greenhouse."

Ms. Carter shook her head slowly. "I still don't understand."

Jeri could see that the house mother thought she'd lost her senses. "I just found a crushed daffodil bulb under Brooke's bed. In their garbage can I found a spoon with salsa and bits of the crushed bulb on it. Daffodil bulbs are poisonous," she explained. "People can get accidentally poisoned when they think a daffodil bulb is a small onion or piece of garlic." She held up her hand. "And when you handle daffodil bulbs without gloves, you get a rash—just like the rash on Brooke's hands."

Emily shrank back from her roommate, pushing herself into the corner of the couch. "Is this true? Did you try to poison me?" Her pale face lost even more of its color. "But why? What did I ever do to you?"

It felt to Jeri as if everyone had frozen. Someone had even paused the movie, capturing a swimmer in the middle of a high dive.

Emily's anguished questions hung in the air. When Brooke just stared at her lap, Jeri said, "I think I can guess. Ms. Todd believes you'll win the science fair with your brain functions display. Brooke tried at Abby's party to make you too sick to work on your project. When that didn't work, she added something during the week to your trail mix. But you recovered again and got back to work. Today's salsa would have made you too sick to answer questions for the judges tonight. That would finally give Brooke a chance to win."

Emily frowned. "But Brooke doesn't care about winning. Just ask her."

"That's right," Brooke said. "I've already got an A in science, and I don't need a scholarship."

Jeri glanced at Ms. Carter, who was watching her as if she'd gone crazy. *Have I?* Jeri wondered. Was her conclusion all wrong? No, it couldn't be! But if Brooke didn't need the grade or the scholarship, why *would* she do it?

"Well?" Ms. Carter finally said.

Jeri shook her head, as if clearing away mental cobwebs. Something didn't add up, but she couldn't put her finger on it. *God, what is it?*

She studied Brooke closely. Her expression was grim, and her arms were folded tightly across her chest. Those tiny tops and tight jeans ... Was she wearing them because they were fashionable ... or because she'd outgrown them and couldn't afford new clothes?

"Brooke, are you sure you don't need the scholarship?" Jeri asked. "Do you really have plenty of money? Then why were you borrowing money from Nikki? I heard her mention loans you didn't pay back." Jeri turned to Ms. Carter. "If you call Brooke's parents or ask the headmistress, you might discover their real money situation."

Ms. Carter studied Brooke thoughtfully, a frown line deepening between her eyes. "Yes, I suppose I could do that." Brooke took a big breath. "You don't need to." Her shoulders slumped, and her breathing was ragged. "Pretty much everything Jeri said is true."

"You *did* poison me?" Emily's voice rose shrilly. "Why? I thought you were my friend!"

"I am!" Brooke's voice caught in her throat. She glanced at her roommate, then away quickly. "I never put enough in your food to really hurt you."

Horror was etched onto Emily's face. "I ended up in the hospital!"

"I know, and I'm really sorry! I don't know how that happened. I must've guessed wrong on the amounts." Her voice dropped almost to a whisper. "I just needed you to miss the science fair." She leaned her elbows on her knees and stared at the floor. Tears ran in thin lines down her cheeks and dripped off her chin. "Jeri's right. My parents' florist shop is almost bankrupt. If I don't get the scholarship for next year, I can't come back."

You won't come back now anyway, Jeri thought. *You'll be expelled.*

Jeri glanced at the girls now huddled silently in the hall. Nikki stood at the back. "Nikki's bigger than Emily," Jeri said, "but she got the sickest at Abby's birthday supper. Why?"

Brooke mumbled so low that it was hard to make out her words. "I don't know. I mixed some poisonous mushrooms in with the good ones from the grocery store when I was in the kitchen."

"But nobody saw you," Jeri said.

"It was while Abby was changing clothes and I was helping you get tea refills. I wanted it to look like a bug that was going around."

Jeri nodded. "It'd be too obvious if only Emily got sick."

Brooke squirmed on the couch. "After we sat down, I knocked over Emily's glass, as a distraction. While Dallas mopped up the water, I added more mushrooms to Emily's salad. I don't know what happened to Nikki."

"I think I do," Nikki said, coming into the room. "I helped clean up afterwards. Before throwing away the leftover salad, I picked out the mushrooms. I love mushrooms. Well, I *did*. Not so much now."

"And I hate mushrooms," Rosa said. "I picked mine out. That explains why I never got sick that night."

Jeri cocked her head to one side, studying Brooke. "I suppose the other incidents during the week were to make it look even more like a virus spreading."

Brooke nodded, and then glanced up at Jeri. "I knew about the daffodil bulbs from my parents' florist shop, but how'd *you* know?"

"Mr. Petrie's book listed poisonous foods, but also flowers—like hydrangea and jonquils and daffodils." Jeri rubbed her sore elbow. "You got the bulbs from the greenhouse, right?"

Brooke didn't move or answer. Ms. Carter touched Brooke's shoulder, and she jumped. "Come with me," the house mother said quietly.

"Wait." Jeri wanted to know one more thing. "What did you add to the trail mix?"

Brooke was silent.

Jeri decided to try a bluff. "Rosa didn't eat hers, but she saved it. We can have the police lab test it."

Brooke sighed. "Dried elderberries."

Jeri frowned. "Elderberries? Those aren't poisonous. My grandma made elderberry jam, and it never made me sick. Grandpa made elderberry wine too."

"Cooked berries are fine." Brooke stole a guilty glance at Emily. "Raw ones are poisonous." Suddenly she cried out, "But I didn't mean to make you that sick! I *didn't*!" She sobbed and couldn't seem to catch her breath. "I th-th-thought you were going to die!"

Arm around Brooke, Ms. Carter led her from the room. Jeri glanced at Emily, then at Brooke's retreating back. The girls in the hall disappeared upstairs. "You okay?" Jeri finally asked Emily.

"I don't know. I still can't believe this! Why didn't Brooke tell me her family was having trouble? I would have tried to help her." A shudder ran through her, and she dropped her head in her hands. "She didn't have to poison me." Her voice was barely a whisper. A moment later she looked up. "I'm sorry I ever thought it was you—or Abby."

"It's okay. You think you can compete at the science fair tonight?"

"I don't know. I hope so. I *have* to!" She glanced at the clock on the mantel. It was 2:40. "By eight o' clock I should be okay." She shook her head. "Well, better anyway."

"Want to come somewhere with us first?" Nikki asked. "My horse show's at four. I think Dallas is coming too."

Jeri nodded. "It might help take your mind off Brooke and all this."

"And relax you enough to perform for the judges," Rosa added.

Emily smiled slowly. "Okay. You convinced me."

The equestrian contest went exactly as Jeri and Rosa had predicted. Nikki took first prize, earning another blue ribbon. In a surprise to them all, though, Nikki gave the judges a letter from her parents, which they read over the loud speaker. It stated that the scholarship should go to the *second*-place winner instead. The applause was thunderous. Looking stunned at the news, Janeen rode her Palomino into the ring to accept it.

Jeri worked hard Sunday afternoon and evening. She finally had the story of the year — and just in time to write it up for the media fair. Only it wouldn't come together. She discarded one version after another.

To make the article outstanding, she needed to report the whole story. But that would mean telling the truth about Brooke and Emily, about Nikki getting poisoned and Abby getting blamed. She knew Emily and Brooke (and their parents) wouldn't want the publicity. The Head might not either. She was finishing her fourth attempt at the article Sunday night when Rosa burst into the room.

"Brooke got expelled!" she said breathlessly. "Her parents have to pick her up tomorrow."

"I can't say I'm surprised," Jeri said, shaking her head. "I thought she might even get arrested. I still can't believe she did that just to win the scholarship."

Rosa flopped down on her bed. "I guess she was desperate."

"Why didn't she just talk to us?" Jeri asked. "We could've figured something out. I guess wiping out the competition was her shortcut to winning."

"While others, like Sierra, cheat to win," Rosa said. She was quiet for a long time. "Well, if you don't have God in your life to help you, you're kind of stuck trying to get things to happen your own way." Rosa smiled with a lopsided grin. "I don't have their excuse though."

"What do you mean? Excuse for what?"

Rosa sat up and wrapped her arms around her bent knees. "Instead of being friends with guys—like you are—I take shortcuts of my own to get attention."

"It takes guts to admit that," Jeri said. "I've noticed the changes you've made already. My mom says God will give us boyfriends when the time is right—someday."

"Ya think?" Rosa hopped off the bed. "I just hope he doesn't take too long!" Grinning, she flounced out of the room.

Laughing to herself, Jeri turned back to her article. Now, where was she? Oh, yes, the news about Brooke. What should she do with the information? Brooke getting expelled *was* news. Could she include it at the end of the article? It seemed mean and unkind—but reporters had to tell the truth.

Jeri leaned back in her chair. Maybe she wasn't cut out to be a news reporter after all. It had been her dream all year, but when her friends were involved, it put her in a tough spot. Should she tell the whole truth or not? If she left out parts that might embarrass her friends, was she a real reporter? Somehow she didn't think so.

Whatever she decided to do, the project was due first thing Monday morning. She'd better decide soon.

Sighing, Jeri wondered why she was making such a big deal out of it anyway. Sierra would probably win with her stunning photo-essay book. Especially if Rosa was right and it really was her *dad's* stunning photo book.

Jeri was up till midnight finishing her front-page article and the final formatting of her newspaper. Back aching, Jeri stretched and rubbed her neck. For better or for worse, the article was done. She'd been as honest as she knew how to be. She only hoped it didn't get her disqualified.

Monday night's media fair found the group of school friends together again, this time lined up in the front row of the auditorium. Jeri was glad Ms. Carter said Dallas could join them—just in case she won! Five finalists would be called up to sit in the five empty chairs on the stage. Mrs. Gludell, the *Lightning Bolt's* sponsoring teacher, and Headmistress Long were already onstage, waiting to do the honors.

Mrs. Gludell cleared her throat. "And now the moment we're all waiting for," she said, smiling down at the audience. "This was an extremely difficult decision to make this year. Several projects were worthy of winning full scholarships." She turned to the Head, who nodded her agreement. "Unfortunately, that's not an option. So ... the other judges and I chose the one girl we felt was most deserving."

Head Long stepped to the mike then. "I will read off four finalists' names. Would those girls please come up onstage at this time?"

Jeri blinked in surprise and glanced at Rosa. Four? Why only four? There were five empty chairs onstage. She held her breath as the Head read off the names: "Cara Thompson, Andrea Williams, Deedee Jones ... and Jeri McKane." Her friends broke into applause as Jeri hurried forward and climbed the stairs to the stage.

Jeri sat between Cara and the empty chair. While people were still applauding, Jeri whispered to Cara, "Where's Sierra Sedgewick? I heard she was probably getting the scholarship."

"Don't you know? She got disqualified!" Cara whispered behind her cupped hand. "Head Long saw some of her photos in a copy of *Photography Today*—with her dad's name on them. She didn't take those pictures in her media project!"

Jeri sat back, mixed feelings fighting inside her. She was horrified for Sierra. She couldn't imagine being confronted by the Head and accused of cheating. But part of her surged with sudden hope too. Maybe her own project had a fighting chance now!

Jeri sat perfectly still and made herself breathe deeply

and slowly. *God, I want your will,* she prayed. *If I still don't win, help me be happy for the winner.*

"May I have everyone's attention, please?" Head Long said, silencing the chattering crowd with "the look." "It gives me great pleasure to award the scholarship to a very commendable young woman." She opened a folder. "The winning student put together a newspaper, complete with an article based on her own investigation of a recent crime on campus. The article ends with some thought-provoking ideas about the pressure students feel to win scholaships—and the lengths some are willing to go to win."

Jeri felt the heat rising from her neck to her face, and she knew she was blushing furiously. She didn't dare look at Rosa or Dallas or any of her friends.

Ms. Long turned and smiled at Jeri, then added, "I would love to read the article aloud right now, but I can't. A police investigation is underway, and they don't want certain information made public. However, I can assure the audience that the article—the whole newspaper—is excellent writing. You'll read it some day. We look forward to Jeri McKane's return next year and her work as a *Lightning Bolt* staff member."

Applause broke out then, and Ms. Long motioned for Jeri to come forward.

Jeri looked down at the front row of chairs as she walked across the stage. On one end waving wildly was Rosa, dressed in a cute skirt that even Jeri's mom would approve of. Emily was next to her, dividing her time between watching the stage and grinning at Dallas, who sat on her other side. Jeri felt a twinge of envy there, but she couldn't blame Emily for liking him.

Jeri did too—and she hoped one day that Dallas would like her back even more. In the meantime, she'd pray about growing into the kind of girl that someone like him would want for a girlfriend. Someday.

We're all just friends, she reminded herself. *For now, that's enough.*